MW00984349

Quilt-Ridden

A Southern Quilting Mystery, Volume 14

Elizabeth Craig

Published by Elizabeth Craig, 2021.

QUILT-RIDDEN

First edition. March 30, 2021.

Written by Elizabeth Craig.

In memory of Daddy, Henry Smith Spann

Chapter One

Beatrice lazily decided there was nothing better than a Sunday afternoon nap after a big meal. She and Wyatt had just eaten a scandalously large lunch that one of their favorite church ladies had foisted on them after the service. Fried chicken, buttermilk biscuits, green beans, and a fruit salad now consumed, she was drifting in and out of hazy consciousness on the sofa. Wyatt was somehow a good deal more alert and was attempting the *New York Times* Sunday crossword puzzle from a book he'd gotten for his birthday. His brow was furrowed with concentration. Noo-noo, their corgi, was napping alongside Beatrice—or, rather, partially on top of her—on the sofa.

Suddenly, Noo-noo struggled up and gave a low growl, peering toward the front door, a crinkle in the middle of her brow. A piercing shriek cut through the air and Beatrice completely woke up, rushing to the door behind Wyatt and Noo-noo to see what happened.

"Did it sound like it came from Miss Sissy's house to you?" asked Wyatt.

"I think so," said Beatrice, although she'd been pretty groggy when it started.

Sure enough, as they quickly jogged into sight of their elderly neighbor's home, they spotted the old woman shaking a broom at their new neighbor, Linton Hoover. Linton was ducking as she swung at him and hollering right back at her as Miss Sissy continued shrieking and brandishing the broom.

Beatrice and Wyatt's other neighbor, local police chief Ramsay Downey, soon joined them. His reading glasses were askew on his nose and he wore an aggrieved expression.

"What in the Sam Hill is going on out here?" demanded Ramsay.

"What's going on is that you need to arrest this woman," spat Linton. "Can't you see she's attacking me?"

Ramsay drawled, "What I can see is that she's on her own property and you are not. That's why I'm asking *you* the question, Linton."

Linton continued staring balefully at Miss Sissy and the old woman shook the broom at him again. Her wiry gray hair had nearly completely tumbled out of her bun and her expression was wild and fierce. Linton, on the other hand, was now quickly composing himself. He ran a hand across his head to smooth down his already-smooth reddish-brown hair as it flopped over his forehead. He gave Ramsay a lopsided, rueful grin.

"Sorry about all the commotion," he said, holding his hands out in front of him to calm down the assembled. "I'll admit I'm on Miss Sissy's property."

"Thief!" growled Miss Sissy.

"I will not, however, admit to being a thief. I came over to see Miss Sissy for the sole purpose of speaking with her about her property. She began to attack me, as you just witnessed."

Miss Sissy bobbed her head in agreement about the attack and made a quick leaping movement toward Linton, which caused him to rapidly back away.

Wyatt had a wonderful way with Miss Sissy and gently approached her. This was good because Ramsay was looking warily at the unpredictable old woman as if he wasn't quite sure how to handle this unusual interruption of his Sunday afternoon.

"What was Linton speaking with you about? What made you upset?" asked Wyatt in a soft voice.

Linton snorted. "Great. Get the minister involved. Is this the way things are run in this town?"

Everyone ignored him except for Miss Sissy, who hissed in his direction, eyes narrowed. After making sure Linton was properly cowed, Miss Sissy growled, "Wants to take my stuff."

Ramsay frowned. "Take your stuff?"

"I said no such thing. I merely asked her to better-manage her property," corrected Linton stiffly.

Ramsay glanced at the looming house next door. Linton had bought the land and tiny home from Piper when she married and moved in with Ash, Ramsay's son. He'd razed the house and built a tremendous home on the lot. Although the sounds of construction and the many trucks on the small country road had annoyed Beatrice, she had to admit Linton had apparently created many local jobs in the process. And, from what she'd heard, the interior of the house was just as fancy as the exterior. Linton had hired a local designer and tried to furnish his home, from all accounts, with goods from local shops.

"What does Miss Sissy's property have to do with yours?" asked Ramsay as if the two things were so vastly different, like apples and oranges.

"It's an eyesore," said Linton in a tone of voice that indicated he was stating the obvious. "You know."

Beatrice looked over at Miss Sissy's house, trying to see it through the eyes of a new neighbor. She'd personally gotten used to it all—the weedy vines and trees that enveloped the home were like something out of *Sleeping Beauty*. Her only concern had really been that Miss Sissy should not be completely engulfed by the rapidly growing brush in the process of entering or leaving the home and getting tripped up in it. She'd never really thought of it as an eyesore, but more of an extension of Miss Sissy in an odd way.

Miss Sissy snorted. "Wants to steal it."

Linton gave a long-suffering sigh and held out his hands in supplication. "Never. I don't want your house. I want it to be tidy."

"*Is* tidy!" bellowed Miss Sissy.

Beatrice realized how relative the word *tidy* could be.

"Perhaps on the inside," said Linton in a clear effort at being diplomatic. "Not on the outside, however. And I've just invested a lot of money and time into my own home and property. Your yard detracts and distracts from mine. I wanted to see if she might be interested in selling her home to me."

"Sneaked into my house," said the old woman in an aggrieved voice. "Did it yesterday or day before. Took my quilt!" The last was said in a holler that could probably have been heard streets away.

Ramsay, clearly irritated about having his Sunday afternoon routine jeopardized, glowered at Linton. "Is that true?"

"I haven't been in her house before a few minutes ago and I certainly didn't steal a quilt at any point. I'll admit that I was inside her home this afternoon. She didn't answer her door. It wasn't locked and I walked right in. For heaven's sake, she's a million years old. It was practically a welfare check."

Ramsay narrowed his eyes at Linton. "In future, please remember that the Dappled Hills police chief lives right down the street. If you need any welfare checks, you can knock on my door."

Linton affected a subdued expression and nodded.

"Took pictures," hissed Miss Sissy.

Ramsay was now becoming increasingly annoyed. "Did you take pictures?"

Linton sighed. "Sorry. Her décor was an excellent example of early Americana."

Ramsay looked doubtfully at him and then poked a finger at him. "Don't do it again. Delete the pictures you took—you were on private property. And leave her alone."

Linton gave Miss Sissy's out-of-control landscaping a regretful look and then nodded and everyone retreated to their own homes.

Wyatt chuckled as he returned to his crossword. "A bit of unexpected excitement on a Sunday afternoon."

"I'll say," said Beatrice. She looked indecisively at the sofa. "I'm not sure if I can summon up the appropriate sleepiness to resume napping."

"Apparently, Noo-noo can't, either." Wyatt glanced over at the corgi who was now sitting by the front door, an alert expression in her brown eyes.

"It was something of a disruption, wasn't it, Noo-noo?" asked Beatrice.

"Linton didn't realize what he'd gotten into when he went inside Miss Sissy's house," said Wyatt, his eyes crinkling at the corners.

"That's for sure. He could have gotten further with her if he hadn't barged right in. She obviously thought he was a burglar."

Wyatt picked up his pencil to carefully write in a crossword answer. "He was lucky. She could have done far worse damage to him."

Beatrice snorted. "He certainly didn't do anything to further a good relationship with Miss Sissy. Next time she might just pick up something more dangerous than a broom." She paused. "I guess I've gotten used to the way her house looks. I don't think I even really *see* the crazy yard anymore, do you?"

Wyatt set his pencil down to consider this. "I wouldn't say I don't *notice* it, but it doesn't bother me. That's just the way Miss Sissy's yard is."

"That's the way I think of it, too. It's irredeemable," Beatrice huffed. "And you know, I don't think I care much for Linton. I know we met him when he moved in, but I was relatively unimpressed. He was very short with us, do you remember?"

Wyatt wrinkled his brow. "I don't think I remember that, no."

"Brusque," said Beatrice. "He was trying to get rid of us."

Wyatt grinned at her. "Maybe he misunderstood the purpose behind our visit. Having the local minister and his wife show up at his door might have made him think we were planning on dragging him off to church with us."

"Better than having the local police chief show up at your door," said Beatrice, her mouth tilting up in a smile. "I'm sure that could be even more alarming."

"Ramsay? Alarming?"

"When he wants to be. Which isn't very often," allowed Beatrice.

There was a knock on the door and Beatrice groaned. "Oh no. What now?"

Wyatt chuckled as he walked to the door. "Well, Noo-noo looks excited so I'm guessing it's Meadow."

Beatrice muttered. "Glad *someone* is happy about having a visitor. Although Noo-noo is probably excited because Meadow is trying to unload all Boris's treats so Boris can lose a few pounds."

Sure enough, Meadow came in pink-cheeked and breathless from hurrying over. "Noo-noo!" she crooned to the little dog and tossed her a couple of treats which Noo-noo happily gobbled up.

Meadow trotted over and plopped down on the sofa where Beatrice reluctantly joined her. Meadow glanced around and said, "Well, doesn't it look all Sunday-cozy here! Newspapers scattered around, a cup of tea on the coffee table. And a crossword for Wyatt! Looks a lot like our house, except for less food."

Meadow was quite a cook and Sundays tended to be her showcase day. Ramsay got to reap the benefits of her cooking bonanza and it was no wonder that he'd been eager to return home after the brouhaha down the street.

Meadow launched right in, as was her usual way. "So what happened at Miss Sissy's? Ramsay was remarkably unhelpful in his explanation. I'd have gone over there myself if I hadn't been in the middle of cooking."

Wyatt said, "Just a little trouble between neighbors. Ramsay resolved it all."

Meadow snorted. "Right. You're attributing too much power to Ramsay, Wyatt. Miss Sissy is like an elephant—she never forgets. And it sounds like she has Linton in her sights."

Beatrice shook her head. "I think you're making a mountain out of a molehill. You know how Miss Sissy is. She gets riled up over very little things. Remember how she got mad when the guild stopped doing the fabric swaps?"

Meadow rolled her eyes. "Do I? She was going to boycott future guild meetings in protest. She had a hissy fit right there in the middle of Posy's living room."

"Same sort of thing here. Linton wanted to talk to her about the fact her property is a disaster and offered to purchase it and Miss Sissy went ballistic."

Meadow's brow furrowed. "Miss Sissy's property is a disaster?"

"You don't notice it now either? I thought it was just Wyatt and me. We've gotten so used to it that I think we were slightly stunned when Linton brought it up."

Meadow walked back to the front of the house and peered out the window. "Goodness. Yes, it is a mess, isn't it?"

"But it's always been that way so we don't even see it anymore. If it were gone, I'm not sure I would even recognize Miss Sissy's house. It's so distinctly Miss Sissy that it's nearly part of her identity," said Beatrice.

"We could pay a few teenagers to clean it up," said Meadow, deep in Save-Miss-Sissy mode. Considering she was still bringing the old woman supper several times a week, she'd been in this mindset for a while.

Wyatt said gently, "We could. But is that what *Miss Sissy* wants? That's what we don't know."

"Why *wouldn't* she want it tidied up, though? There are vines everywhere and even a couple of volunteer trees really close to the house. She couldn't possibly see out of her windows. And it's so dark inside. If we just had someone cut it all back, it would brighten things up," said Meadow.

Beatrice said, "That all makes a lot of sense, Meadow. But you have to remember that Miss Sissy doesn't actually make sense."

Wyatt added, "And she just threatened Linton with bodily harm for suggesting she needed to clean her property up."

"Well, that's true," said Meadow, the fervor to clean up suddenly gone. "I suppose Miss Sissy doesn't want saving. Or maybe she actually likes her house that way. *Did* she threaten Linton, then? Ramsay just said there was an altercation. It's nearly impossible to get information from him these days. Especially on a Sunday."

Beatrice said, "Oh, she was threatening him. With a broom, which I suppose was what was handy. She brandished it at Linton quite fiercely."

"I can picture that. Totally. Linton was lucky he got away without any bumps or bruises."

Beatrice said, "I think *Miss Sissy* was lucky. If Linton had gotten whacked with her broom, he'd have pressed charges, for sure. I halfway thought he was going to press Ramsay to arrest her when we first got there."

Meadow bubbled with laughter. "What Linton doesn't know is that Ramsay wouldn't have wanted the paperwork. He never would have arrested Miss Sissy because he wanted to go back to his reading and writing and Sunday snacking." She suddenly clapped a hand to her forehead. "Oh gosh, I completely forgot. Ramsay got some wonderful news."

Chapter Two

Beatrice's eyes opened wide. "About his writing?"

"Exactly! He won the regional short story contest and now he'll be entered into the state competition. Isn't that wonderful?" Meadow beamed as Wyatt and Beatrice agreed. Then she looked serious. "Oh, but you can't tell anyone. He wanted me to keep it a secret."

Beatrice rolled her eyes. "Meadow! You shouldn't have told us."

"Well, I had to tell somebody and I know you two can keep a secret. Even though I apparently can't. The regional folks wanted to keep the winner under wraps until they announce it at the fair, but wanted to make sure Ramsay was going to attend the fair to accept the award."

Wyatt said, "I'm glad you said something to us. Beatrice and I will want to make sure we're there when the winner is announced so we can clap and cheer for him."

Meadow gasped. "That's true. Wouldn't it be awful if everyone was on the carousel or in line for cotton candy and no one applauded?"

"I don't think that's likely to be a problem," said Beatrice. "After all, that's the main stage. There should be plenty of folks there."

"Yes, but for the *music*: the local bands that are playing. They may not hang around for short story winners. Then poor Ramsay would be walking up on the stage, proud as punch to get his award, and it will be completely silent." Meadow's face was a study in horror.

"But it *won't* be that way. Wyatt just pointed out that we'll be there cheering him on." Beatrice felt a small headache coming on.

"Maybe I should let Posy and Cork know," mused Meadow. "And just a couple of others. People who'll be sure to keep this information under their hats."

Wyatt and Beatrice exchanged a look. It was Dappled Hills. Keeping information under hats was not the modus operandi.

Wyatt decided to change the subject before Meadow planned to erect a billboard in the town announcing Ramsay's win. "How is Will doing? I know he had an earache yesterday. Is he feeling any better?"

Meadow's expression immediately changed to her fond, mothering look. "He's an absolute angel. His ears were *much* better when I saw him yesterday afternoon, the little love. He's not tugging on them at all. And he didn't cry a bit. He's the most perfect grandbaby in the world."

Beatrice smiled at Wyatt as Meadow waxed poetic about their mutual grandchild for a while. Will was definitely a safer subject. And Beatrice had to agree with Meadow on at least one point—Will was certainly remarkable in every way.

Meadow seemed to be wrapping up her soliloquy on Will's many virtues as a baby. "Then, when he woke from his nap, I heard him stirring and walked in and he gave me the most adorable smile! It was the cutest. Ash used to wake up really fussy from naps, but Will is always so cheerful and good-natured. But of course, you both know this, too! You're part of the Will Downey fan club, the same as me."

They chatted amiably about the baby for a while before Meadow started circling back to the fair again. Beatrice skillfully detoured Meadow's attention from Ramsay to quilting since the quilters would have exhibits in the crafts area.

Meadow abruptly said, "Oh, I know what I forgot to mention. You know Bertha Cooke, don't you?"

An image came to Beatrice's mind of a woman with a pleasant smile, a hearty laugh, and shoulder-length curly brown hair. "I don't know her well, but I know who Bertha is."

"As you know, she's a quilter," said Meadow.

Beatrice raised her eyebrows. "Actually, I didn't know that little tidbit."

"Well, she is. She doesn't have much time for guilds, though, since she works a lot. She's a housekeeper for half the town, it seems. I think she took over a lot of homes when June Bug started the bakery. Anyway, she's self-taught and comes from a long line of quilters. She has some very old quilts in her home and offered to speak at our next guild meeting and show them off." Meadow beamed.

Beatrice felt a prickle of interest. As a retired museum curator, this was exactly the sort of thing that fascinated her. "That's fabulous, Meadow. I'll look forward to seeing those quilts."

Meadow sighed. "I did try to recruit her as a Village Quilter again, but it was a no-go. She apparently is just really booked up with cleanings. I do think that has the potential to be a really tough job, don't you? For one thing, just creating order out of people's messes. For another, having to deal with obnoxious people."

Wyatt looked a little bemused. Meadow seemed quite strident on this point, which wasn't much like Meadow. She was usually aggressively cheerful. Beatrice asked, "Who in particular were you thinking of? Did she mention who she cleans for?"

Meadow made a face. "Who knows? But I have to imagine that her usual clientele would be someone like Linton. Can you imagine putting up with someone like him as an employer? He sure sounds like he's pushy, if he was trying to make Miss Sissy do what he wanted."

"Perhaps he's better with people who work for him," suggested Wyatt mildly.

"Hmph," said Meadow in an unconvinced voice. "He'd better be. Ramsay told me last week he'd even gotten into a brawl with Dan Whitner. He'd been called to the bar outside of town, but by the time Ramsay made it there, Dan and Linton had already left. Separately, I'm sure. Apparently, they were mad as anything."

Beatrice tilted her head to one side. "Dan Whitner. Isn't he painting the Patchwork Cottage right now? I could have sworn that that's who Posy said when she introduced him when I was there."

"Exactly," said Meadow triumphantly in the tone of someone who was proving a point.

Wyatt and Beatrice exchanged glances again. If there had indeed been a point made, they were both uncertain what it had been.

Meadow charged ahead, oblivious of their confusion. "See what I mean? He's not an easy person to be around and now he's our neighbor! He's brawling with Dan Whitner, a mild-mannered odd-jobs guy. He's fighting with Miss Sissy, a petite little old lady . . ."

"Now you're taking this a bit too far," said Beatrice dryly. "From what I saw, Miss Sissy was about to beat Linton within an inch of his life."

"Regardless," said Meadow, "the point is that he's difficult. Maybe he's mean to Bertha, too, since she cleans for him. We should keep a close eye on him. Who knows what will happen next?"

Having aired all her grievances and worries, Meadow was now even more full of energy. "I do enjoy catching up with you, Beatrice! It seems like we don't have as much time for idle conversation now. Oh, we *see* each other when we're handing off our darling Will between us. But we're always talking about the baby and how he's doing and less about our own things."

Wyatt gave Beatrice an amused look. Of course, it was Meadow who was doing most of the talking about Will on any occasion.

"Let's have a coffee tomorrow," said Meadow impulsively. "No, a *breakfast*. Come by tomorrow morning about 7:00. Just us girls. Sorry, Wyatt! I'll get rid of Ramsay. No, never mind, he'll get rid of himself. He's always scribbling in his notebooks first thing in the day anyway."

Beatrice's first impulse was to come up with an excellent reason why she couldn't make it. But, as she tried to find a perfect excuse, she realized that there wasn't one.

"That's not too early, is it?" asked Meadow. "It's just that I'm trying to get Boris back on an exercise schedule. We were doing so well and then we had a busy couple of weeks and everything sort of fell apart. I figured we could have coffee and breakfast and then I could take Boris on a walk."

Boris was their tremendous, good-humored beast of a dog. Exercise was a priority for him, not only because the vet was worried about some weight gain, but because he became even more mischievous than usual when he wasn't regularly walked.

"No, that's fine. Thanks, Meadow," said Beatrice grudgingly as a smile tugged at Wyatt's lips.

"Great!" said Meadow, slapping her knees before standing up and heading for the door. "Well, I'll leave you both to your quiet Sunday afternoon." She cast a bemused eye over the puzzles and books and Beatrice got the idea that Meadow's own Sunday afternoon would be significantly more active and boisterous.

Beatrice released a sigh of relief after Meadow closed the door behind her.

Wyatt grinned at her. "Now, it won't be that bad. You know that Meadow's breakfast will be mouth-wateringly delicious."

"Oh, I know. I feel bad about not wanting to go. I do usually end up having a great time once I get there. It's just that Meadow can be so exhausting."

"Maybe you'll enjoy something of a grace period from Meadow after you get a proper visit in," suggested Wyatt.

"Let's hope so," said Beatrice as she settled down on the sofa with Noo-noo and her book and soon drifted off into a peaceful nap.

The next morning, Beatrice got dressed and took Noo-noo for a short walk. She glanced at her watch and called out to Wyatt, "You're leaving in the next few minutes for that appointment, right?"

He poked his head around the bedroom door and gave her a wry look. "You know me too well."

"I know you strongly dislike doctor appointments," said Beatrice with a grin. "You don't ordinarily run late for anything, but you're seriously dragging your feet this morning."

"I'll be in the car in two minutes," promised Wyatt as Beatrice gave him a peck on the lips and then headed out the door to walk to Meadow's house.

Meadow and Ramsay lived in a converted barn that was somehow made to feel extremely cozy, despite the lofty ceiling. There were quilts everywhere and the aroma of baking lingered in the air. Boris greeted Beatrice joyfully at the door but thankfully didn't jump.

Beatrice took a deep breath. "Muffins?" she asked, a hopeful note in her voice.

"Blueberry," sang out Meadow.

Beatrice gave a sigh of contentment as she sat down at the kitchen table. These were Meadow's very own blueberries that she grew on their property. The morning was starting out very promising, indeed.

"How are things going over at your house?" Meadow carefully slid a bacon and cheese omelet onto a plate with hash browns and then put the plate in front of Beatrice along with a cup of fresh coffee. "Go ahead and eat while it's warm."

"Oh, things are going pretty well. I did nearly have to use a crowbar to get Wyatt out of the house for his physical, but that's par for the course for doctor appointments for him." Beatrice ate a forkful of omelet and closed her eyes briefly. It was absolutely perfect. She was going to have to figure out why her own attempts at making omelets went so poorly.

Meadow chuckled. "Ramsay is the same way. I have to make all his appointments for him or he'd never go to the doctor at all. He has high blood pressure and we're supposed to be monitoring it at home. I have to force a cuff on him every day. Considering he's the police chief, he's such a baby."

Meadow put the blueberry muffins on the table, fixed her own plate, and joined Beatrice. They spent the next few minutes blissfully consuming some very excellent breakfast food.

"Did I mention to you that Ramsay is speaking to a group of aspiring authors at the library?" asked Meadow finally.

"That's not supposed to be a secret, is it?" asked Beatrice dryly. "Like the award he's getting at the fair for his short story?"

"Silly! Of course not. It's a public event and in the library's newsletter. He's going to be giving advice about starting a writing habit."

Beatrice took a sip of the freshly-squeezed orange juice that Meadow had given her. "He'll be perfect for giving that talk. When I see him, I'll tell him so. He's been writing for years. And he reads several books a week. I'm sure he'll have plenty of wisdom to impart."

Meadow looked worried. "I know he will. I just hope there'll be a few people there at least. I can't imagine that Dappled Hills is just covered up with writers. Maybe we should plan on being there, for moral support." She chuckled. "I swear I fuss over Ramsay as if he was a child of mine. I guess I must not have enough things to worry about so I have to worry over him."

"You care about him, that's all. You're looking out for his feelings."

Beatrice was about to finish off the first of what she hoped would be several blueberry muffins when there was a frantic knock at the door.

Boris exploded into barking, leaping at the door.

Meadow's brow furrowed. "Who on earth could that be? It's rather early for a social call, isn't it?"

"Well, technically, *I'm* here for a social call," said Beatrice. Since Meadow seemed to be more interested in speculating who could be at the door than actually answering it, Beatrice slipped Boris's harness over his head with some difficulty and pulled the huge animal back from the door as she unlocked it and pushed it open.

She recognized the woman who stood there but only because she cut a very glamorous figure around Dappled Hills. She had large, green eyes, black hair, and was fond of wearing upscale black clothing and red lipstick. Ordinarily, of course, she didn't look panicked, but she did now. Beatrice stepped back so that she could come in.

Meadow had stood and apparently could do more than simply recognize the woman who'd arrived at her house. "Sandra

Hughes!" she said. "Goodness. Do come in. Has something happened?"

Boris was continuing to bark and generally cut up, as if determined to be as raucous as possible after his extremely demure welcome of Beatrice earlier. Ramsay surfaced from the back of the house, reading glasses pushed up on his forehead and a bemused look on his face. "What in the Sam Hill is going on?" he asked.

Sandra immediately hurried up to him. "It's Linton," she said abruptly. She impatiently wiped a stray tear from her cheek. "He's dead."

Chapter Three

Meadow gaped at her. "Linton?" she repeated shrilly. "Linton, our neighbor, Linton?"

Meadow always had the notion that neighbors and quilters should never, under any circumstances, be in any sort of trouble whatsoever. She was continuously horrified that this never seemed to be the case.

Ramsay started striding for the door with Sandra, Meadow, and Beatrice following. "No," he said to them quickly. "Stay here and I'll be back soon. Where was he?" he asked Sandra grimly.

"The games room," she said in a hoarse voice.

Ramsay blinked for half a moment at the mention of a games room, but then hurried back out the door.

Sandra started pacing around Meadow's kitchen.

"Coffee?" asked Meadow anxiously, although it was clear to Beatrice that Sandra needed something to calm her down, not something to wind her up more than she already was. "Muffins? They're my own blueberries."

Sandra appeared not to have even heard her at all. "I'll step outside to smoke."

Meadow said, "We'll come with you."

Out on Meadow's patio, Sandra pulled out a cigarette with shaking hands, lit it, and puffed away as if it were going to deliver her from her current situation. Her hands continued trembling as she smoked.

Beatrice observed that Sandra appeared to be in no mood for conversation but had the feeling Meadow wasn't going to be able to help herself.

Finally, Meadow, after several minutes shifting from foot to foot, exploded into questions. "What happened, Sandra? What did you see? Is Linton really gone? Should I call an ambulance?"

Sandra looked at her coolly as she blew out a puff of smoke. "I walked into the house and called for Linton. He didn't answer. I looked for him. I found him. He was dead." She shrugged a thin shoulder and quickly took another drag on her cigarette.

"In his *games* room?" Meadow was apparently stumped by this—either by someone actually possessing a games room, or someone perishing in one, or both.

Sandra nodded.

"Was it . . . well, did he have a heart attack or something? A stroke? Some sort of horrid medical event?" Meadow was clearly desperate to make this an unfortunate natural episode.

Sandra shook her head. "He was murdered. With a pool cue. In the games room."

It sounded very much as if she were playing a game of *Clue*. But her demeanor suggested that she was a lot more upset than her words indicated.

They were quiet for a couple of minutes, watching Sandra smoke and pace on the patio. Meadow couldn't contain herself any longer and asked, "But what were you doing there? Isn't it awfully early for a visit?"

Sandra gave her a small smile. "I'd have thought you'd, if anyone, would have known Linton and I were dating. The rumor mill in Dappled Hills must be broken."

Meadow blinked at her. "You and Linton?"

Sandra's small smile grew, despite everything. "You can't picture us as a couple?"

"Not very easily," admitted Meadow. "He seemed so abrasive."

Sandra gave a short laugh. "That was Linton, all right. But he wasn't *always* abrasive. He could be quite kind." Now she blinked rapidly to dispel what Beatrice suspected were tears in her eyes.

After Sandra's cigarette was over, Beatrice wondered if she was going to start another one. It seemed to cross Sandra's mind too, but then she hesitated. "You did mention coffee." She looked at Meadow.

Meadow was delighted to fall back into the familiarity of hostess mode after the confusion of the last few minutes. "That's right—and blueberry muffins! And an omelet, sausages, hash browns . . ."

As Meadow continued listing the bounties of her breakfast table, Ramsay came back in, a grim expression on his face.

Meadow blurted, "Well? What happened, Ramsay?"

"I have my deputy there to guard the scene and the state police are on the way."

Sandra, seemed to pale a bit more, although her skin was such a light shade of porcelain that it was hard to tell.

Ramsay said, "I do need to ask you some questions, Sandra."

She stiffened and then gave a bob of her head.

"Maybe Meadow and Beatrice can head out on the patio for a few minutes," said Ramsay.

"That won't be necessary," said Sandra, lifting her chin slightly. "I have nothing to hide."

Ramsay gave a nod of acknowledgment and took out a small notebook from his pocket. "You could start by telling me everything that happened this morning."

He took a seat at the breakfast table and Sandra hesitantly did too. Meadow quickly piled a plate with food and poured a large cup of coffee and slid them in front of her. Sandra took a deep breath and started. "This morning? Well, there's not a lot to tell. I was at home until I drove to Linton's house. The morning was like any other morning—I ate some cereal, walked on the treadmill for thirty minutes, and clearly didn't have nearly enough coffee to face my day. Then I hopped in the car to drive to Linton's."

Ramsay scribbled a few notes. "You and Linton were in a relationship, is that right?"

Sandra gave a shaky laugh. "That's right. For some months."

"And when you arrived at the house, there obviously wasn't an answer when you rang the bell? Or did you just walk in?"

Sandra took a long sip of coffee and then another before answering. "I rang the bell. Then I knocked. Then I figured that Linton was running water somewhere in that huge house where he couldn't hear me, so I walked in and called his name."

Ramsay jotted more notes and then nodded to her, encouragingly. Sandra took a deep breath.

"There was no answer, so I started looking for him."

"Did you usually meet up early in the morning, or was this a special thing?" asked Ramsay.

Sandra looked down at the plate of food in front of her as if assessing the question. "Well, we tried to. Sometimes Linton had all the best intentions in the world and then overslept." Her voice broke on the last few words and she put her hand to her mouth, regaining her composure.

Ramsay looked steadily at her, waiting for her to be able to speak again. A few moments later, she did. "Anyway, we'd decided to meet up this morning. Part of me suspected I'd walk in there and wake Linton up again because he'd overslept."

Ramsay nodded as he wrote a few more notes. "Was it usual for Linton to leave his door unlocked like that? Even overnight?" His voice suggested he thought this was a very bad idea.

Apparently, Sandra agreed with him. She snorted. "Sadly, yes. Linton thought Dappled Hills was the very definition of safe."

Meadow bubbled up again. "Of *course* it is!" she exclaimed, despite all the evidence to the contrary.

Ramsay gave her a wry look and then turned again to Sandra. "So you walked in, calling his name."

Sandra rubbed her arm absently. "That's right. He didn't answer, so I kept looking. The games room was the last place I looked. I mean, if Linton *had* been up early, the last thing he'd have been doing would be to play pool or any games. But there he was." She paused and then looked directly at Ramsay. "And I saw that he'd been struck over the head with a pool cue. It was obvious it was foul play."

"So you ran over here to let me know," said Ramsay.

Sandra gave her head a slight shake. "First I checked on Linton. Just to make sure he wasn't just unconscious and needing medical help."

"Of *course* you did!" said Meadow, giving Ramsay a look in case he had any objections to Sandra potentially disturbing a crime scene in some way. "You'd want to help him, if you could!"

Ramsay gave Meadow something of a quelling look and then said kindly to Sandra, "And you found that he didn't need any help."

Sandra lifted her chin again and seemed to be working to keep it from trembling. "He was already cold. I was careful not to disturb him in any way. Then I hurried off to find you."

Ramsay nodded.

"Is it *murder* then, Ramsay?" demanded Meadow.

Ramsay said, "Yes. But I need all of you to keep the information about the manner of Linton's death to yourselves, please. Nothing to anyone about the pool cue." He looked sternly at Meadow and she clapped a hand over her mouth.

He turned again to Sandra. "I know this must be a terrible shock for you. But we have to do what we can to bring Linton's murderer to justice. I'm sure he would want that. Do you have any ideas about who could potentially be responsible for Linton's death?"

Sandra tightened her lips for a minute. "Well, I think there are plenty of possibilities. After all, Linton was a very wealthy man and an influential one. People were jealous of him . . . that's only natural."

Beatrice didn't necessarily think that was the case. Of all the talk she'd heard about Linton, it was mostly either derisive or irritated and had to do with the size of his house and how it didn't really fit in with the other houses on the street. Or perhaps his inability to fit in with the rest of Dappled Hills, although he'd apparently grown up there before moving away and then returning.

Ramsay looked thoughtfully at Beatrice as if he could read her mind. Then he said to Sandra, "I can understand that. Was there anyone in particular who seemed to have a grudge against Linton?"

There was a flicker in Sandra's eyes for a moment before she looked down at her hands. Then she said, "Well, there's Heidi Wheeler."

"Farmer Aiden's wife?" Meadow gaped at her. "But she seems like such a sweet, gentle girl."

Beatrice hid a smile. *Farmer Aiden* sounded like someone out of a children's storybook. It made her wonder if she ever referred to other people that way. Police Chief Ramsay? Pastor Wyatt?

Sandra cast her an irritated look. "Sometimes people aren't exactly what they seem, Meadow."

"In what way?" asked Ramsay, giving Meadow another frown.

Sandra sighed. "It was very evident to me that Heidi had something of a crush on Linton, regardless of whether she was married to the good farmer or not."

Meadow stared at her.

"She was very jealous of Linton's and my relationship with each other. And she'd lurk around Linton's house, hoping to run into him."

Ramsay said slowly, "That's interesting. I don't think I ever noticed her there."

"But she did it. And then when he'd come out, she'd just *happen* to run into him on her walk."

Meadow tilted her head to one side. "On a walk? But Heidi doesn't live anywhere near here."

Sandra gave a condescending smile. "That's exactly the point. She parked in downtown Dappled Hills in her nicest clothes and took a walk from that point. I'd think if you lived on a farm that you'd be able to find plenty of exercise on your acres and acres of property. Wouldn't you think? Like I said, she had a crush on him."

Beatrice asked, "What was Linton's reaction to Heidi's infatuation?"

Sandra shrugged. "Just what you'd expect. He wasn't interested. Oh, I'm sure he was *flattered*. I mean, it's not everyday that a grown woman has a crush on you, is it? And Linton was *polite* to her. He wasn't the sort of person to be cruel. But he was going out with me and was sure to tell Heidi that."

Beatrice noticed that Sandra's color had risen in her cheeks a little, creating a faint blush of pink on her white face. Was she lying? Or was she just agitated from her irritation over Heidi's infatuation?

Ramsay crinkled his brow. "All right. But if Heidi cared so much about Linton, why would she murder him?"

"Rejection," said Sandra. "When you're rejected by someone, it can really make you snap. She wanted to be with Linton. Maybe she wanted to leave her husband for him or would have. How do I know what was going through her head? But she'd have been turned down and maybe she just couldn't stand the idea of going through life seeing Linton around town and knowing he could never be hers."

Sandra was starting to look antsy again and Beatrice wondered if she were craving another smoke. Ramsay seemed to pick up on this, too.

"Got it. Well, I'm sorry for your loss, Sandra. You've had a terrible shock and should probably head home and take it easy for a while. Let me get your cell phone number in case the state police or I have additional questions later on."

Sandra gave it to him and left, looking relieved.

Ramsay shoved his notebook in his pocket and stood up. "I'll need to go back and join the state police. Beatrice, did you happen to see anything odd going on at Linton's house on the way over here for breakfast? A car over there or somebody hanging around who didn't belong? Or did you see Linton, even?"

Beatrice considered this for a moment and then shook her head regretfully. "I'm afraid not. I was thinking about other things. I like to think I would have noticed if I'd seen Sandra over there, but I didn't."

"It's all right," said Ramsay. "You didn't know that anything had happened over there, after all." He sighed heavily. "I suppose I'll have to go speak with Miss Sissy."

Meadow erupted. "Miss Sissy? You can't possibly think Miss Sissy would have anything to do with this."

Ramsay raised both his hands as if protecting himself from the onslaught or perhaps trying to calm Meadow down. "Now, Meadow. You know very well that Miss Sissy needs to be spoken with. She just had an extremely animated altercation with Linton yesterday."

"Because he broke into her house!"

Ramsay snorted. "You know he did no such thing. Her door was unlocked and he walked inside. Saying he broke in was just Miss Sissy's melodramatics at work. I have to rely on what I saw and what I heard. What I *saw* was Miss Sissy threatening Linton with bodily harm."

"With a *broom*," scoffed Meadow.

"And what I heard," said Ramsay, "was Miss Sissy accusing him of being a thief. She was very worked up."

"Miss Sissy is *always* worked up," said Meadow, rather worked up herself.

Ramsay made a calming gesture. "I'm not going over there to arrest Miss Sissy, Meadow. But I would be remiss if I didn't go speak with her after what happened yesterday afternoon. Besides, she lives directly next door. She might have seen or heard something."

"Then take us with you," said Meadow, straightening up with the idea. "Let her think it's something of a social call so you won't hurt her feelings. I'll bring some of the leftover breakfast."

Ramsay opened his mouth to object, then shut it again. "Actually, that's not a bad idea. I won't get much from Miss Sissy if she's in a bad mood. And food always makes her happy."

Meadow beamed. "Then it's decided." She bustled over to the stove and loaded a plate full of food, wrapping it carefully in saran wrap. "Let's go."

Chapter Four

Miss Sissy's house was the same as it had always been, but Beatrice noticed the wildness of her grounds this time. It was funny how quickly she'd been able to overlook them and almost attribute them to an extension of the old woman, herself. Ramsay, Meadow, and Beatrice made an interesting group as they walked up the broken walkway to Miss Sissy's front door: Ramsay still managing to look official and grim, Meadow plastering on a big grin, and Beatrice clutching the plate of food Meadow had thrust at her to give the old woman.

Miss Sissy answered the door, peering suspiciously around it at the trio. Her eyes lit up greedily when she spotted the plate of muffins, omelet, sausage, and hash browns, though, and she hastily ushered them in, leaving the door wildly ajar as she headed inside, leaving Beatrice to shut it carefully behind them as they followed her in.

Beatrice blinked in the dim light of Miss Sissy's home. It was filled with dark, old wooden furniture and very old quilts. Miss Sissy favored heavy curtains that blocked out most of the light, even on the sunniest of days. And the home, like the outside of it, was rather untidy.

Ramsay, who'd spoken briefly with the state police as he'd passed Linton's house, was trying to manage something of a neighborly tone, despite serving in an official capacity. He watched as the old woman grabbed the plate from Beatrice and attacked the food with gusto. Finally, he cleared his throat and said gently, "Miss Sissy. We did want to check on you and bring you some breakfast. But we also needed to speak with you about your neighbor, Linton."

Miss Sissy scowled at him.

Ramsay continued mildly, "You were having an argument with him yesterday."

"Taking my stuff," growled Miss Sissy before popping another forkful of food in her mouth.

"What stuff did he take?" asked Ramsay. "When I saw him, he didn't seem to have anything in his hands. Was it small enough to fit into a pocket?"

Beatrice marveled at Ramsay's patience. Glancing around at Miss Sissy's grim furnishings, it seemed hard to imagine that Linton coveted something of Miss Sissy's. Especially enough to risk life and liberty to break in to take it.

"Didn't steal it then," acknowledged Miss Sissy gruffly. "Was coming back for more."

Ramsay tilted his head to one side thoughtfully. "Okay. So Linton had come to your house previously and stolen something? He was back on your property to take *more* things?"

Miss Sissy gave a fervent bob of her head in agreement and more of her wiry gray hair tumbled out of her precarious bun.

"What did he take the first time?"

"A quilt," hissed Miss Sissy.

Beatrice glanced around again. The house was crammed full of quilts. Not only had Miss Sissy been quilting for most of her considerable years, but her mother, grandmother, and forbears had all quilted. How could she possibly tell that one was missing, especially in this chaotic environment?

Ramsay appeared to share Beatrice's concern. "Are you sure about that, Miss Sissy? You're sure the quilt isn't misplaced? Or that it's not just underneath another quilt?"

Meadow gave Ramsay an exasperated look. "For heaven's sake, Ramsay! Miss Sissy has an amazing mental inventory of all of her quilts. I've always been impressed that she knows exactly what patterns are represented, who quilted them, and where they're located. If she says one is missing, one is missing."

Ramsay took a deep, calming breath. "Right. So let's say Linton did take one of your quilts, Miss Sissy. He mentioned yesterday that the only reason he'd come over here was to tell you that he wanted your property kept up a bit better. Or maybe to purchase your property from you."

"Thief!"

"Maybe we should let Miss Sissy eat for a few minutes," suggested Beatrice. "It might be easier for her to have a conversation after her tummy's full."

Meadow beamed at her. "An excellent idea, Beatrice."

Miss Sissy gave Ramsay a miffed look and proceeded to eat the rest of her breakfast in silence. Ramsay, who needed to join the state police next door, fidgeted and stole peeks at his watch from time to time. Meadow, never one to enjoy silence, started an animated conversation with Beatrice about the upcoming fair and how she'd bought an adorable new outfit for the baby to wear to it.

"Do you think he'll be big enough to ride on the carousel?" asked Meadow.

Ramsay gave her a shocked look. "Absolutely not."

Beatrice hid a smile at his overprotectiveness. "Only if we're on the horse too and hold him on."

In just seconds, Miss Sissy polished off the rest of the food. Beatrice was never quite sure where the calories even settled on the old woman's thin frame. She gave Ramsay a reproving look but folded her hands in her lap and gave every appearance of now being ready to cooperate.

Ramsay gave a relieved sigh. "So, the missing quilt. Why do you think Linton would take it?"

Miss Sissy narrowed her eyes at him as if not believing he could be so dim. "For money!"

"Okay," said Ramsay hastily. "So it's a valuable item, is it?"

Miss Sissy gave an irritated sigh and looked over at Meadow and Beatrice for help.

"Of *course* it is! Why else would Linton steal it?" demanded Meadow.

Ramsay looked up at the ceiling as if trying to locate his lost patience there. "What I'm asking is why Linton would want to steal a quilt at all. It certainly didn't seem to fit in with his modern décor."

Beatrice said slowly, "Maybe he wanted to sell it. After all, that was quite an expensive house to construct and furnish. And, from what I hear, he's been living large here in town. Could he have been shorter on funds than we realized?"

Ramsay nodded. "That's definitely something we'll have to follow-up on." He turned back to the old woman who lifted her chin defiantly. "Now, Miss Sissy, your neighbor unfortunately died this morning."

Miss Sissy looked unsurprised at this news, as if she considered Linton likely to be dead for any number of reasons.

Ramsay explained further. "He was murdered, as a matter of fact."

A spark of interest lit in Miss Sissy's eyes.

"Which means I'm afraid I have to ask you where you were this morning and what you were doing and if anyone can verify it."

Meadow gave an exasperated sigh.

Miss Sissy growled, "Was here at home. Nobody saw me."

Ramsay turned to Beatrice and Meadow. "Neither of you did?" he asked, hopefully.

They both shook their heads regretfully.

Ramsay looked dejected. "All right."

Meadow said impatiently, "She lives by herself! Who was supposed to give her an alibi? How would she have known she needed one?"

Ramsay changed the subject slightly. "I tell you what, Miss Sissy. Maybe you can help out by telling us if you saw anyone over at Linton's house this morning. Anyone at all."

Miss Sissy glared at him and pointed at her windows. They were indeed covered with heavy drapes.

"You didn't peek out the window at all?" asked Ramsay in a hopeful tone.

Miss Sissy's scowl deepened as if that was a ridiculous suggestion.

"I think we're done here, aren't we?" asked Meadow, standing up and taking the empty plate from the old woman.

"I suppose so," said Ramsay. "Do be careful, Miss Sissy. If there's someone dangerous running around, you'll want to make sure you keep your doors locked and windows closed."

Miss Sissy demonstrated that she did indeed listen to his suggestion when they left. She locked the door behind them quite vehemently.

Ramsay quickly disappeared to join the state police next door and share his findings. Meadow grabbed Beatrice by the arm. "We've got to figure this out!"

"What—you mean Linton's murder? Ramsay looks like he's getting a good start on doing that," said Beatrice, pulling her arm away none-too-gently.

Meadow rolled her eyes. "But you know how Ramsay is. He's very deliberate. And . . . well, his investigations just seem to take forever. You, on the other hand, are able to get to the bottom of things much more quickly."

"Only because I don't do anything in an official capacity. I don't have a bunch of red tape holding me up. Ramsay has to make sure his I's are dotted and his T's are crossed."

"That's exactly what I mean! You're a natural. And you need to get started asking questions. Otherwise, Ramsay and the state police are going to keep looking at Miss Sissy as a suspect." The horror of this made Meadow grimace.

Beatrice shook her head. "My plans this morning involve going to the Patchwork Cottage."

Meadow grinned and gave Beatrice a thumbs-up. "Perfect! Good thinking, Beatrice."

Beatrice frowned, trying to piece together her brilliance in running a necessary errand to pick up batting for her latest project.

Meadow continued, "After all, Dan Whitner is there painting the shop for Posy."

Beatrice, who'd endured a very confusing morning, continued frowning.

Meadow finally explained a little more. "Remember? Dan is doing odd jobs for Posy. But he also was in a bar fight with Linton Hoover!"

Beatrice nodded. "Oh, right. I'd forgotten that part. Well, I suppose it wouldn't do any harm to speak with Dan while I'm over there." She glanced at her watch. "I really do need to get back now, though."

"We still have tons of breakfast food left."

Beatrice patted her tummy. "My stomach thinks I'm done, though. It feels very full; I guess the food has already hit it and told my brain I'm done. Maybe that's a trick I should try every day—pause in the middle of a meal for a while."

"Okay, but I'm bringing you some of my leftover blueberry muffins at some point."

"Meadow, that sounds *perfect*."

Beatrice walked back to her house and let Noo-noo out. The sun was shining brightly and Beatrice tilted her head up for a moment to feel its beams on her face. When she and the little dog came back in, her phone was ringing.

Wyatt was on the other end and his voice sounded plaintive.

"What's wrong?" Beatrice felt her muscles tense up. "Did the doctor find something wrong?"

"He found that I needed to lose a little weight," said Wyatt with a sigh. "I guess I've been eating a little too well."

"Oh, well, if that's all. I think we can deal with that."

Wyatt said glumly, "I suppose so. It just doesn't sound like much fun. My metabolism must be really slowing down or else I'm eating far too many calories. He gave me a bunch of different options to try, in terms of dieting. None of them sounded particularly appealing. But I think I might try the one where I try to eat just whole foods. Edgenora was telling me about it and it sounds easy enough. And it's supposed to be higher in fiber and vitamins and minerals."

Edgenora was the church administrative assistant. Beatrice knew she had an iron will and quite an amazing ability to stick to a regimen. The diet *sounded* like one of those things that was easy, but the application of it could be hard. Beatrice said, "Whatever you'd like to do . . . I'm onboard. I'll join you."

Wyatt quickly said, "You don't need to do that. You haven't picked up any extra weight."

"But it will be easier if *both* of us do it. Besides, it sounds like a healthy thing to do. I could stand to eat a little healthier. You can imagine how I ate at Meadow's today. It was absolutely *delicious*, but it wasn't exactly health food."

Wyatt said, "Only if you want to. No pressure." But his tone had lightened a little at the thought of not taking it on alone. "How has your morning gone?"

"I can't believe I haven't mentioned it yet—I guess I got all distracted worrying about how your appointment went." Beatrice told him about Sandra interrupting her breakfast with Meadow, Linton's death, and the subsequent visit to Miss Sissy's house.

Wyatt's voice was serious on the other end of the line. "Oh, no. I'm sorry to hear about Linton. Is Ramsay considering Miss Sissy as a suspect?"

"Well, I guess he's not exactly in a position not to, unfortunately, especially taking into account what happened yesterday. But I don't think he seriously believes she had anything to do with it. You didn't happen to see anything over at Linton's house this morning when you left for your doctor appointment, did you?"

Wyatt said regretfully, "Not a thing. I was more focused on the road ahead of me. I don't think I even glanced over across the street at all."

"I'm the same. I went right past there on my way to Meadow's, but never took a look."

Wyatt said, "Be careful today. That's awfully close to home."

"I have Noo-noo to protect me," said Beatrice lightly. The little dog, hearing her name, lifted her head and gave her open-mouth grin at Beatrice, game for anything, even if she wasn't exactly sure what she was signing up for. "But of course I'll keep a close eye out. Right now, I'm getting ready to head to the Patchwork Cottage to pick up some supplies."

Wyatt said slowly, "I'm pulling into the church parking lot—and I'm seeing Brett Hoover's car here."

Brett was Linton's brother. He did portrait photography and event photography and was taking photos that week for the church's pictorial directory that came out every few years. "Oh, no."

"Do you think Ramsay has had the chance to tell him about his brother?" asked Wyatt.

"No, I doubt it. He was going right back over to Linton's house to meet with the state police there. Maybe you should give Ramsay a quick call and let him know Brett's there and ask him what to do. Word is sure to spread quickly, and he doesn't need to find out from one of the church members."

Wyatt quickly hung up to call Ramsay, and Beatrice left for the Patchwork Cottage in downtown Dappled Hills. As she walked into the shop, she felt her spirits lift as they always did as soon as she entered. It was a happy place full of cheerful music, lovely quilts, and a range of fabric that set her creative juices flowing. Just now, the shop was in a bit of disarray because of the painting Dan Whitner was doing—he was refreshing the buttery yellow of the walls and so the quilts that usually filled them had been carefully taken down and put into storage for the time being. Posy gave a cheerful wave to Beatrice as she finished checking out another customer's purchase.

Beatrice got her batting and then couldn't resist a quick look at the newest fabrics. She was especially drawn to one in particular that looked like it would make the perfect quilt for Will. The little boy was fascinated by a dinosaur picture book that Ash and Piper had been reading to him and this fabric had cartoon-like dinosaurs all over it, doing improbable activities like playing baseball.

"Getting tempted?" asked Posy with a twinkle in her eye.

Beatrice chuckled. "You know me well. And it's not like Will doesn't have tons of blankets, but I was thinking this fabric would make a nice bigger-boy blanket."

They chatted for a few minutes and then Dan called out from his ladder, "Did I hear right? Is Linton Hoover dead?"

Chapter Five

Posy's eyes grew huge. "Linton? But I just saw him yesterday. He seemed totally fine."

Small towns really did spread news quickly. "I'm afraid so," said Beatrice. "Although I'm a little surprised the word has gotten out so quickly."

Dan carefully applied some paint to the wall. "It probably hasn't much, yet. I only know because my girlfriend told me about it. Bertha cleans for Linton and was told by the police that she needed to stay away when she got over there a little while ago." He turned around and gave them a somber look. "She reckons it was murder, what with all the cops there. Said it wouldn't have been that many cops if Linton had just had a heart attack."

"Mercy!" said Posy, shaking her head. "What on earth could have happened? Do you think it was a break-in that went wrong? I know he has a nice house with a lot of nice things."

Beatrice said, "I don't really know." Maisie, the store cat, came up to Beatrice and rubbed lovingly against her legs. Beatrice reached down to pet her and the cat affectionately bumped the top of her head against Beatrice's hand.

Dan was focused back on his painting again and talking cheerfully away. "It could be a break-in, sure enough. Bertha says the house is real fancy. But I hear Linton didn't get along well with a lot of people." He colored. "I got in a fight with him, myself, at the bar not long ago. He was a sorta condescending fella. But I was out of town last night and just came back in this morning—came straight here. So I had nothing to do with any kind of trouble."

Posy looked a little taken aback at the thought of her mild-mannered painter engaging in bar fights in his off-hours.

Beatrice said, "You said he didn't get along well with lots of people. Was there anyone in particular you had in mind?"

Dan used a stick to stir the paint, thoughtfully watching it swirl. "His own brother didn't even get along with him great. And you know what a good guy Brett is. I don't think Brett could stand Linton. I heard Brett talking about Linton down at the bar."

Posy, always the peacemaker, said thoughtfully, "Maybe that was just a sibling thing? Sometimes brothers don't always get along."

Dan nodded. "True, that. But this was a little more than just brothers getting irritated with each other. This was over money. I couldn't hear everything Brett was saying, though." Dan looked regretful.

Maisie padded off to the sofa to curl up and take a nap. Beatrice, as she paid for her batting, made a mental note not to say anything around Dan that she didn't want the whole town to know about.

As Beatrice climbed into the car, her phone immediately started ringing. Wyatt was on the other end. He sighed. "Today has already been a very strange day."

"What happened with Brett at the church? Did Ramsay come over to tell him about Linton's death?"

Wyatt said, "He did. Ramsay asked me to stay close in case I could offer any pastoral help after Ramsay told him. But Brett didn't. He just looked very solemn, nodded his head, and then continued setting up his equipment at the church for the photographs. It's likely how he handles grief, which everyone approaches differently. But I feel terrible having him working here at the church today. Every member of the congregation is going to know about his brother's death in no time and he'll be having to speak with them all about it as he's taking photographs."

Beatrice said, "It will be okay. Maybe he wants to keep busy. And if he doesn't like talking about his brother over and over, he'll go home."

She could tell Wyatt was still concerned about Brett and said, "You know, I actually needed to run by the church office anyway and pick up a few things. How about if I check in on him there?"

Wyatt sounded relieved. "Would you? I have to head off for the hospital to make a couple of visits, otherwise I'd do it myself."

"It's no trouble at all."

The church was actually another of Beatrice's happy places, so it really *wasn't* any trouble. She always felt calmer and more at peace as soon as she stepped on the grounds. The church was a couple of hundred years old with ivy scaling the beautiful old stone walls. The grounds were brightly-colored with rhododen-drons and azaleas and there were birds singing everywhere since volunteers strung up feeders and birdhouses and kept the bird-baths filled.

She first went by the church office to check her mailbox there and then headed to the church hall where the photos were being taken for the directory.

Brett Hoover was considered something of a ladies' man in Dappled Hills, although Beatrice wasn't sure if that was just wishful thinking on behalf of the town's women. He was tall and handsome with dark, wavy hair. He usually had a kind of smirk-ing smile on his face, although it was understandably absent to-day. He lifted his hand in a quick wave of greeting to Beatrice as he took a family picture of a husband and wife with two small girls who were very wiggly. He rapidly shot a couple of more photos and then ushered the family out. The next person hadn't arrived yet, so he had a short break and strode over to see Beat-rice.

"I'm so sorry about Linton," said Beatrice.

Brett gave a short nod. "Thanks, Beatrice. I'm sorry, too. I just wish I knew what happened. I couldn't believe it when Ramsay told me."

"I know Wyatt has encouraged you to go home for the day. I think it might be a good idea. Edgenora and I could easily call everyone and reschedule their photos. People would understand and it's no bother for either of us."

Brett gave her a wry look. "Isn't it? I don't know—I sort of feel that calling twenty-five people, playing phone tag with some of them, would add a lot of hassle to your day." He paused and his eyes grew gentler as he noticed Beatrice was trying to figure out the best response. "Sorry. I appreciate the thought, but I have the feeling that I'll do a lot better simply working through this today. If I were at home, I'd be totally restless. At least here I can get my work done."

"Can I get you anything? Pick something up at the store? Something to eat or drink?"

He shook his head. "No, thanks. I think I'll be all right. I brought a coffee in with me this morning and that's probably all I need." He gave a short laugh and pushed his dark hair out of his face. "I must sound really cold, staying at work and everything."

Beatrice shook her head. "We all react to grief differently."

He sighed. "It's just that my relationship with Linton wasn't all that easy. We were never all that close, even as kids, and Linton didn't do a lot to make us any closer. We grew up here, but then Linton moved away for years. Then, of course, he moved back in the last year to Dappled Hills. Did you know him at all?"

Beatrice thought back to what she'd heard about Linton and how he'd acted with Miss Sissy. She shook her head again. "I'm afraid I really didn't. We were neighbors, of course, but I haven't reached out as much as I should have."

"No, *Linton* should have reached out. That's the thing—that's the pattern that Linton always followed. He only really thought of himself. That's awful to say, but it's the truth. After Ramsay told me what had happened, he asked me if I knew who might have wanted to murder Linton. I told him 'who doesn't?'" He gave a bitter laugh.

Beatrice said softly, "I'm sorry. It sounds like it was a tough relationship."

"Oh, it was. Of course, I wouldn't have lifted a finger against Linton. For one thing, I never won a fight with him and I knew better than to start one. And, as I told Ramsay, there were other people far angrier with Linton than I was." He glanced quickly at the door to make sure they were still alone and said, "Aiden Wheeler, for one."

"The farmer," said Beatrice.

Brett's mouth curved up in a smile. "Exactly. He's a great guy, but I have the feeling he wasn't too happy to find out that his wife was having an affair with Linton."

Beatrice's eyes widened a little. Sandra had said that Heidi was only flirting with Linton, not having an affair with him. And that Linton had rejected her, making her angry.

"It's true. Linton told me himself," said Brett. "He only had himself to blame for this whole thing."

Beatrice said slowly, "But I thought Linton was dating Sandra Hughes."

"He *was*. But that didn't stop him from seeing Heidi and trying to juggle two relationships at once. See what I'm saying? There are plenty of people who might have wanted Linton dead." He frowned and said as an aside, almost to himself, "I guess I'm going to have to figure out the service for Linton and everything. Is Wyatt still here at the church?"

"Actually, he had to go make his hospital visits. I can get him to run by as soon as he's done, though."

Brett said, "Don't worry about it—I'll catch up with him sometime tomorrow. This service is going to be cut-and-dry, anyway, if I even have one at all. It shouldn't take much planning."

An elderly lady poked her head tentatively around the door of the church hall and Brett quickly called out, "You're in the right place! Come on in." He smiled at Beatrice and said, "I'll see you later."

Beatrice hopped in the car for the short drive back home. She glanced over at Linton's house and saw there was still a team of police in forensics gear there and loads of different vehicles. She winced and headed inside her own house.

She felt unsettled after the unusual morning. Although she wasn't really hungry yet, she decided maybe a small snack and a cup of tea was in order to help her get oriented back into her day again. As Noo-noo watched her with interest, she put some salted, roasted pecans in a small bowl and then made a cup of chai tea. She put far too much sugar and cream into the cup, but figured she was due a treat after a tough day.

As the tea steeped, she gazed thoughtfully into the cabinets at the food there. Although she was currently about to enjoy a healthy snack, she saw a *lot* of processed food in the cabinets. She made a face at it. She and Wyatt both hated waste, so she just put the crackers and chips into zipper bags to try and keep them fresh and put them out of sight in the coat closet where they wouldn't be tempting either of them. It might well be harder to take on this diet than Wyatt had supposed. And it was definitely going to mean a trip to the grocery store later for fresh fruits and vegetables.

There was a knock at the door and Beatrice peered out the front window to see who it was. She smiled as she saw Savannah

Potter wave a tentative hand at her. Savannah was a friend and a fellow quilter with a rather awkward manner, but a kind heart. She bicycled everywhere, preferring not to drive.

"Good morning!" said Beatrice, opening the door.

Savannah, who always strove to be accurate and correct, glanced at her watch. "Afternoon, I believe," she said with an apologetic smile.

"Wow," said Beatrice. "That morning passed by fast. Come on in. I was just making myself a snack . . . would you like one?"

Savannah's eyes radiated gratitude. "I'd love one, thanks, Beatrice."

Beatrice headed back into her kitchen and then paused. "What kind of snack would you like? One of the healthy ones that I'm eating? Or would you like some of the cornucopia of junk food that I have in a cabinet?"

Savannah said in her very serious manner, "Some of the cornucopia of junk food."

"Good. In fact, would you like to take it with you? Wyatt is trying to eat healthier and I thought it might be best to keep the junkier stuff out of sight." Beatrice pulled out some cheesy crackers, cookies, and chips and gave Savannah a hopeful look.

Savannah's shoulders slumped and Beatrice frowned. "What's wrong? Did something happen?"

Savannah blew out a sigh and said glumly, "Not really. Well, yes, but not in the way that you mean. Georgia's and my aunt has come into town and is staying with me. She's determined to cook very healthily while she's here."

Beatrice brought the food over to the table and set it down in front of Savannah before heading back to the kitchen for a plate, napkin, and water. "Is it just that she's looking after you? Trying to make sure you're eating right?"

"Oh, she is. I understand why she's doing it, but it's really wearing on me. She means well and she's very nice, of course," said Savannah in a hurry, looking guilty for saying anything negative.

Beatrice sat down with Savannah and watched as she doled out some barbeque potato chips onto the plate and took a brooding bite. "This aunt—she's the one who raised you, is that right?"

Savannah nodded and swallowed down the chips. "That's right. Aunt Tiggy took us in after our parents died when we were young teens. We're very grateful to her and she really stepped up to the plate at the time. But having her stay with me is completely exhausting."

"The healthy food?"

Savannah nibbled on another chip. "The food would be all right if it wasn't *broccoli*. I really just can't stand broccoli and she doesn't season it at all. Actually, she doesn't season *anything* at all. Nothing tastes good nor even like it should. She cooks the vegetables for hours and they fall apart when you try to spear them with your fork." She gave Beatrice an apologetic grimace. "Sorry. I've been over at Georgia's so often to complain that I figured I should try to give her a break for once and bug someone else instead."

"That must be very stressful," said Beatrice gently. She was unused to seeing the always in-control Savannah at a loss.

"Aunt Tiggy means well. But with the food and the fact that she's messy, it really has been stressful."

Beatrice hid a smile. Savannah's definition of messy was different from most people called messy. Savannah qualified as a neat freak and always kept her things carefully labeled and organized. If Aunt Tiggy left as little as a coffee cup in the sink, Savannah probably winced.

Savannah seemed to read Beatrice's mind. She took a sip of her water and said, "I know what you're thinking, but she really *is* messy. What's more, she's making matching dresses for Georgia and me and there's fabric and thread and scissors and things scattered all over the house."

"Maybe she can stay with Georgia for a few days?" suggested Beatrice.

Savannah's face looked hopeful. "Do you think so?" It fell again. "I couldn't ask Aunt Tiggy to do that. Not in a million years. Her feelings would be so hurt that I wanted her to leave. I'll just have to keep escaping and going to friends' houses until she decides she needs to head back home."

"Not necessarily," said Beatrice. "You could ask Georgia to invite her over. Maybe Georgia could tell her that she'd like to spend more time with her or that she could use a little help around the house. Almost as if she was asking your aunt for a favor."

Savannah brightened again. "That's a great idea. I'll call Georgia as soon as she gets back from teaching school." She stood up and looked longingly at the junk food. "I wish I could take these home, but I doubt Aunt Tiggy would approve."

"Could you put it all in a tote bag with some of my fabric scraps on top? Then it would look like a project in progress."

Savannah beamed at her. "You're brilliant today, Beatrice. Actually, I guess you're probably brilliant all the time, but especially so today. I'll just keep the food in my room and grab it whenever I need a snack. Thanks so much."

She headed for the door and then frowned and turned around. "I might be out of it, but why are there so many police cars on your street? Did something happen?"

Savannah at this point might be the only person in Dappled Hills who *didn't* know. Beatrice told her about Linton and she crinkled her brow. "That's awful. Although I suppose he wasn't the nicest person. I was out on my bike one day and he deliberately splashed through a huge puddle with his car right next to me. I was drenched!" Savannah's mouth was a thin line of displeasure.

"Did he apologize?"

Savannah's eyes flashed. "Not at all. And when I caught up to his car at a red light and was fussing at him, he completely ignored me. Even though his window was down and he could hear every word. He just turned his music up."

Beatrice's opinion of Linton Hoover was growing lower and lower as time went on. Still, though, he hadn't deserved to lose his life, no matter how annoying he'd been.

Savannah's thoughts seemed to follow the same track. "I hope Ramsay catches who did it, though. I hate to think that this person is running around loose in Dappled Hills."

"Ramsay will," said Beatrice firmly.

They talked about other things for a while, including Savannah's little gray cat, Smoke. Georgia had made an entire wardrobe for Smoke. Savannah dressed him up daily and took pictures of him, which she shared with Beatrice on her phone.

"I should get Georgia to make Noo-noo a bow for her collar," said Beatrice thoughtfully. "She'd look so cute in one."

Noo-noo, hearing her name mentioned, lifted her head up to look curiously at Beatrice before grinning her corgi grin.

After a while, Savannah left with a tote bag full of carefully-disguised junk food hanging off her bike's handlebars. Beatrice headed out to the grocery store to replenish her stock of healthy food. She was in the produce department trying to remember if it was honeydew melon that Wyatt liked or cantaloupe when she heard someone clearing her throat behind her. She turned to see Heidi Wheeler (or, as Meadow might have put it, The Farmer's Wife) standing somberly behind her.

Chapter Six

Beatrice smiled at her. "I'm sorry, Heidi—am I in your way? I was deep in thought, I'm afraid."

Heidi was a small woman in her early-thirties with brown hair and large, expressive brown eyes. Beatrice suddenly realized that she must be twenty or more years younger than her husband, Aiden.

Heidi gave her an apologetic smile in return, but her eyes were anxious and she looked pale and unwell. She said something in a low voice and Beatrice cupped her ear to indicate that she couldn't hear her.

Heidi said a bit louder now, "No, I'm sorry. I just—well, I was hoping to speak with you. About what happened this morning."

Beatrice nodded and said softly, "About Linton's death?"

Heidi seemed to turn even paler and Beatrice, who had no desire to see her hit the floor of the grocery store, quickly said, "Why don't we go outside for a minute and sit down for a breath of fresh air? Neither one of us has any food in our carts yet."

Heidi gave her a grateful look and followed Beatrice outdoors. The old-timey grocery store had a porch with three rocking chairs. Unfortunately, the rocking chairs were nearly always occupied by a pack of elderly men in baseball caps who chatted with each other daily as they drank their coffee and muttered to each other for hours. They were there again now and looked startled to see Beatrice looking down at them.

"We'd like to sit down, please."

They glanced at each other with confusion.

"Right now, please."

Two of them slowly rose and the third stayed rooted in the wooden rocker.

"It's a private conversation," said Beatrice sternly and the man joined the others, muttering to themselves as they dispersed—likely to sit outside the diner, which was another favorite gathering spot.

"Thank you," murmured Heidi, a faint blush of color in her cheeks now. "Sorry about that."

Beatrice sniffed. "Don't be sorry. These chairs don't have their names on them, although you'd think they did, considering how often they take root here. Please, take a seat."

They sat in the comfortable rockers with the soft, plaid cushions attached. They rocked for a few moments quietly while Heidi appeared to be gathering her thoughts. Then Heidi said in a low voice, "I know Wyatt is technically the person I should be speaking with. I mean, considering he's my minister and everything. It's just that I feel more comfortable speaking with you." Her brow crinkled. "Is that all right? I mean, do you mind?"

Beatrice said warmly, "I don't mind at all and I can promise you that I will keep whatever you tell me confidential, just as Wyatt would. You can rest easy on that." Then she felt a faint ping of worry that maybe Heidi was going to make some awful confession of some kind. She told herself if that was the case that she'd just encourage her to go straight to Ramsay.

Heidi took a deep breath. "Well, I feel terrible admitting this." Her faint blush deepened and she paused as a customer hurried into the store. Then she said quietly, "I had a . . . relationship with Linton."

Beatrice tried not to look like she'd already heard the news. But she didn't want to look as if she found the confession shocking, either. It was a hard balance to make. She just nodded silently, making sure there was no expression of judgement on her face.

Heidi continued, her voice shaky. "I know it was wrong. There's really no excuse at all for having had an affair with Linton. I'm married to Aiden and he's a good man. He's always been kind, always been supportive. He's a hard worker, he doesn't drink, and he's very gentle with me. Like I said—there's no excuse. I strayed because . . . well, I guess because Aiden is so much older than I am. Again, I don't want to excuse my behavior, but explain it."

"You don't have to explain yourself to me," said Beatrice firmly.

Heidi quickly added, "And thanks for that, but I really feel I want to offer some sort of explanation. I don't want you to think Aiden has been a bad husband, because he hasn't. But he and I have very little in common. I was very young when we married and he just seemed so *safe*. He's always provided well for me. But we don't enjoy the same music, the same movies, or even the same food."

"And with Linton, it was different?"

Heidi's eyes brightened thinking about it. "Definitely. For one thing, Linton was so unpredictable. Aiden has such a regimented life. Maybe farmers all have to be that way to fit everything in. He gets up at the same time each day, eats the same breakfast, puts his coffee in his travel mug, and heads out to the cows. His day follows the same pattern. He comes in for lunch, carefully takes off his boots, eats fried chicken, mashed potatoes, and green beans, then heads out again."

Beatrice, thinking it over, decided in many ways that it sounded like Wyatt and her. Substituting Noo-noo for cows, perhaps. And she realized she found this kind of life very satisfying and comforting, especially because of the daily regimen. But she nodded to Heidi and acted as if she understood where the problem lay, even if she didn't totally see it.

Heidi continued, "And Linton? He was all over the place." She chuckled, remembering. "He'd sleep in until noon or wake up at 4 a.m. for the day. Or he wouldn't even go to sleep at all. He'd exercise in his home gym or skip it for a week. He'd be a gentleman or he wouldn't. You wouldn't ever know exactly which Linton you were going to see when you were with him."

That, to Beatrice's way of thinking, made Linton rather defective, but she gave Heidi an encouraging smile.

"Linton and I liked the same books and the same movies. I didn't much like his music, but I loved hearing new stuff for once and music that was so completely different from what I'd usually listen to. Or what Aiden would listen to." She shifted in the rocker and looked away from Beatrice. "I was alone a lot of the day while Aiden tended to the livestock and the crops we had. Farming is a full-time job; at least, it's a full-time job the way Aiden does it. Sun-up to sundown. I had things to do, myself—chores, of course. Cooking. But nothing that I really put any value in and nothing that I looked forward to. I found myself spending more time away from home just so I wouldn't be alone. And then I found myself spending more time with Linton. Our relationship started very naturally."

Heidi looked anxiously at Beatrice. Beatrice said kindly, "I can see that it did. But I do want to ask you something. Sandra Hughes came to Meadow's house while I was there and reported Linton's death."

Heidi straightened in her rocker a bit and gave a stiff nod.

Beatrice said with a sigh, "She seemed to think that she and Linton were part of a relationship."

There was a fierce note in Heidi's voice. "She was just confused. They had an affair and it ended, but Sandra didn't want to believe it was over. She was convinced Linton was going to come back to her, but Linton had absolutely no plan to do that. He didn't even *like* Sandra." This last bit was said with a sob.

Beatrice fished around in her purse for her packet of tissues and handed it to Heidi. She gratefully took one and blew her nose. "Sorry," she said, muffled by the tissue. "I didn't mean to sound so mad. I thought . . . well, I thought you were the one who found Linton. I know you were his neighbor. Somebody told me it was you."

Beatrice shook her head. "No. Maybe someone saw me outside of Miss Sissy's house or speaking with Ramsay and that's what they thought. Sandra had walked into Linton's house, looking for him, and discovered him."

Heidi was quiet for a few moments. "That sounds like Linton—leaving his door unlocked. Because I know Sandra didn't have a key."

"That's what she said—that she just walked in."

Heidi stuck with her story. "Which was exactly what Linton didn't want. All he wanted was to avoid Sandra and be with me. I keep thinking maybe Sandra confronted Linton again and he told her he didn't want her chasing after him anymore. Sandra has a real temper—you do not want to cross her. She could have flipped out when he told her it was over and killed him. Then she could have come and gotten you and made it sound like she'd only found him. How did she look when she came over to Meadow's house?"

Beatrice remembered Sandra's shakiness, her smoking outside on Meadow's patio. She also remembered Sandra talking about how rejection could make a person snap. Could she have been speaking about herself? "She was upset. But she seemed to be upset because someone she cared about was gone, not because she'd murdered him."

"Sure," said Heidi impatiently. "Sandra could *also* have been upset because she wasn't thinking it through when she killed him and was grieving him. She probably regretted her actions. But that doesn't mean she wasn't the murderer."

Beatrice moved on. "Did you and Linton have any sort of a plan? With your relationship, I mean?"

Heidi immediately replied, "We were going to get married, of course. He and I were in love with each other. I felt terrible for Aiden. I hated the idea of hurting him or of making him feel uncomfortable when he drove into town and saw the two of us together. But it also wasn't fair to him for me to see Linton behind his back. So Linton and I were making plans."

Beatrice still felt as if Linton was perfectly happy with life the way it was, but she certainly wasn't going to tell Heidi that. She wondered if Heidi had realized, on some level, that Linton wasn't going to marry her. "What are you going to do now?"

Heidi's eyes filled with tears and she blinked them back impatiently. "What *can* I do? I guess I have to pick myself back up and keep on going. Keep moving forward."

"With Aiden?"

She nodded. "There's no point in hurting him now. Not with Linton gone."

Beatrice asked, "This might seem like an odd question, but did you happen to see a quilt at Linton's house? I know he didn't seem to be a quilt person."

"Why do you ask?"

Beatrice quirked an eyebrow. That seemed like an odd way of responding to a fairly direct question. "Well, his neighbor, Miss Sissy, has a quilt missing and she's pretty upset about it. She blames Linton because it's missing."

Heidi snorted. "The wacky old lady who lives next door to him? She can't be all that reliable, can she?"

Although Beatrice often thought Miss Sissy wacky, she straightened her spine and said in a chilly tone, "Miss Sissy is perfectly capable of knowing when something is missing from her house." She wasn't entirely sure this was true, but felt protective of her friend.

"I'm sorry—of course she is," said Heidi in a rush. "I don't know why I said that. I guess it's all the stress right now . . .

things just come leaping out of my mouth. And no, I haven't seen any sign of a quilt at Linton's house. And she thought he had it? You're right, it just doesn't seem like anything Linton would be interested in."

Beatrice gave a shrug and a quick smile. "She wasn't sure what happened to it, but thought Linton had expressed an interest in the quilt." Which wasn't exactly how Miss Sissy had put it, but was somewhat accurate. "Do you know if Linton had any financial worries? Anything like that?"

Heidi's brow furrowed. "You think Linton took her quilt because he wanted to sell it?"

"I just don't know. I only know Miss Sissy is very agitated about losing it and I was trying to find out what might have happened."

Heidi shook her head. "No, there's no way he'd have done something like that. Linton was really wealthy. Well, you're his neighbor—you've seen his house and cars and things. I don't know if you've ever seen the inside of the house, but it's pretty amazing. He didn't spare any expense at all with the furnishings. The chairs and sofa are totally luxurious. There was amazing artwork on the walls, too. And you wouldn't believe how nice the master bathroom is." She colored a bit and looked away.

But this only emphasized to Beatrice that Linton might have spent a lot of money in a short period of time. A person can be wealthy and still manage to overspend and squander that money. Linton obviously had an eye for nice things and might have spotted something at Miss Sissy's that he realized was valuable and which he assumed she wouldn't miss in all the clutter.

Of course, if this was true, it didn't do much to absolve Miss Sissy from being a suspect in his murder.

She noticed that Heidi seemed to be waiting anxiously for Beatrice to say something. Beatrice cleared her throat and said, "I appreciate your talking this through with me, Heidi. Did it help at all to talk about Linton?"

Heidi gave her a shy smile. "It sure did. And I'm sorry about taking you away from your shopping like that. My head and my heart have just been so full and I haven't had anyone to talk to."

Beatrice said slowly, "I'm good as a sounding board, but I don't know if you wanted me to offer any advice."

"Oh, I do. If you have any to offer."

Beatrice said, "I think it would be a good idea to continue this conversation, but with Wyatt, who's trained in counseling. Or, if you're uncomfortable doing that, with another counselor of some kind. Are you sure you're going to be able to return wholeheartedly to a marriage with Aiden when you were so close to leaving him?"

"I don't think it would be fair to Aiden, otherwise. Like I said, he's a good man," said Heidi.

"Yes, but do you think you could potentially use some couple's counseling to improve your relationship? For both your sake and his?" asked Beatrice.

Heidi hesitated. Then she said, "I'll think about it."

"Good."

They walked back into the store to do the shopping they'd abandoned, but it felt a bit awkward now. Heidi thanked Beatrice again, said a hasty goodbye, and set off toward the other end of the grocery store as if it weren't big enough in there to keep running into Beatrice again . . . which they proceeded to do several times. Beatrice was relieved when the errand was finally over and, healthy food in hand, she set off back home.

Noo-noo was happy to see her and bounced around while Beatrice put the groceries away. Beatrice did some quick housework before deciding to take Noo-noo on a walk to clear her head and give the little corgi exercise after leaving her at the house for a while.

When Beatrice put her in her harness and opened the door, though, she gasped when she saw Miss Sissy's droll features staring directly at her.

"Miss Sissy! You scared the life out of me." Beatrice put her hand over her heart. Noo-noo was too startled to bark or even lie down for a tummy rub.

Miss Sissy glared at her. "You scared *me*!" she insisted.

Beatrice took a deep, calming breath. "I was just about to take Noo-noo for a walk. Obviously. Would you like to come with me?"

Miss Sissy was not a huge fan of taking walks now that she was no longer driving. That's because walking was now more of a form of transportation than it was pure exercise. She scowled at Beatrice and shook her head.

"All right. Well, come on inside then. I don't want to disappoint Noo-noo so how about if I take her for a quick walk and you wait for me in the house. Will that work?"

Miss Sissy considered this. "Snacks?" she asked gruffly.

Beatrice winced. She shouldn't have given *all* of the junk food to Savannah. Miss Sissy wasn't exactly the celery and hummus type.

"There's some food in the fridge," offered Beatrice before quickly ducking out with Noo-noo.

When she returned home, she saw a gloomy Miss Sissy sitting at the kitchen table with a slice of cheese. "What happened?" she demanded.

Beatrice said brightly, "Oh, you mean the healthy food?"

Miss Sissy nodded and her gray hair bobbed around her head.

"Wyatt is trying to eat better and I'm trying to help him."

Miss Sissy made a face to indicate what she thought about the poor judgement involved in this decision. And Beatrice had the feeling Miss Sissy blamed her directly for it. She'd always had a sweet spot for Wyatt and sometimes thought Beatrice got in the way somewhat.

"Where's the baby?" she asked, her gaze darting around the room as if Beatrice might have him hidden under blankets somewhere.

Meadow and Beatrice shared babysitting duties, although Meadow was fond of encroaching on Beatrice's time because of her obsession with her grandson and his alleged brilliance. "He's actually with Meadow this afternoon while Piper is at the school getting caught up on some work."

Miss Sissy did not take this news well. So far, Beatrice had completely struck out with the old woman—no good food and no baby.

"Let's go get him," she barked.

Beatrice quirked an eyebrow. "From Meadow's house? Are you suggesting kidnapping, Miss Sissy? Because I don't think that will go over well with Meadow. And you know her husband just happens to be the police chief."

"Bah!"

Beatrice said, "We could do other things, though. You could help me figure out the best way to cook some of the food I picked up at the store. Maybe you and I could comb through my old recipe box."

Miss Sissy apparently wasn't very impressed with this idea.

"Or we can do some quilting. I have a couple of projects I need to finish up or I won't have anything again for the 'sew and tell' time at the guild meeting."

Miss Sissy yawned.

"Or I could ask you about your missing quilt," said Beatrice.

This finally got the old woman's attention. She leaned in closer. "It's gone!"

Chapter Seven

"Yes, I got that part. What I'm interested in is hearing what your quilt looked like."

Miss Sissy gave her an impatient look as if all quilts looked pretty much the same . . . flat with colors on it.

"Did it have any defining characteristics?" pushed Beatrice. "Do you know much about its history or who created it?"

It was like pulling teeth, but finally the old woman was able to begrudgingly offer some information about the missing quilt. She brightened up a bit as she spoke, giving small details, and was clearly very fond of it, despite the numerous other quilts in her cluttered house.

"So let me reiterate," said Beatrice. "Your quilt sounds very old. It was your great-grandmother's?"

"Great, great," said Miss Sissy with some hostility as if Beatrice hadn't been paying attention.

"I see. So we're talking about the late 1880s or so. And there were a variety of materials incorporated in the quilt: silk, satin, ribbons. And it exhibited some needlepoint work."

Miss Sissy nodded.

"It certainly sounds like a Crazy Quilt to me. And those are fairly valuable. A collector might pay five thousand dollars for one," said Beatrice slowly.

"Mine!"

"Yes, of course it's yours. And you want it back," said Beatrice soothingly.

"Not to sell. To keep."

"Well, it's a family heirloom of yours. Naturally you want to hold onto it. I'll talk to Ramsay about it soon and see if he's found out anything," said Beatrice.

The phone rang then and Beatrice pulled it out of her pocket. "It's Meadow now, actually. Maybe she has some news."

"Get the baby!" reminded Miss Sissy.

Beatrice made a hushing gesture to the old woman and then said, "Hi, Meadow."

Meadow sounded very keyed up. "Are you at home?"

"Yes. Did something happen?"

"I think I broke my ankle. Or maybe I sprained it. I wasn't even *doing* anything, just putting Will in his high chair." Meadow sounded vexed over the misbehaving ankle.

"Do you want me to drive you to the doctor?" asked Beatrice.

"No, Ramsay's able to come by and pick me up. But I do need you to watch Will for me."

Miss Sissy, apparently able to hear the conversation from where she sat, clapped her hands.

"Of course I will. Want me to run over with the stroller?" asked Beatrice.

"No, no, Ramsay will drop off Will. He has a lot of equipment, you know. I simply can *not* figure out how I did this to myself." Meadow's annoyance was growing as time went on. "Arghhh! And Boris has a vet visit today."

Miss Sissy's face fell at the mention of Boris. Although she loved Noo-noo, she wasn't as fond of the overwhelming Boris. She was much more of a cat person altogether.

Beatrice tried to calm down Meadow remotely. "All right. Settle down, Meadow. It won't help anything for you to be frazzled. Just sit down and wait for Ramsay. I'll call the vet and cancel the appointment for today."

"Can you reschedule it? He's got some vaccinations he's supposed to get. And I was hoping to see that Boris has maybe lost a pound or two. I've really cut back on his treats."

From what Beatrice had seen, it wasn't the treats that were the problem. It was the fact that Boris was tall enough to counter-surf and sample Meadow's delicious cooking, himself.

"I'll try to reschedule it as soon as possible. But there's no reason to scramble to try to get him over to the vet today with everything else going on."

Meadow groaned again. "Oh, Ramsay's here already! Heavens! I haven't even pulled together a bag for Will." And she abruptly hung up.

Beatrice put her phone back in her slacks pocket and looked over at Miss Sissy. Her eyes were dancing with glee. "Get to babysit," she said with great satisfaction.

A minute later, there was a thudding knock on the front door and Miss Sissy spryly dashed over to yank it open. Ramsay stood there, holding a confused-looking Will with one arm and a box of various baby paraphernalia in the other.

"Wasn't sure what to pack so I threw everything in the box," he said grimly.

Miss Sissy plucked the baby out of Ramsay's arms and set him over by the baby toys Beatrice had quickly pulled out on the living room rug. He babbled happily and Miss Sissy beamed at him as he played.

"Is Meadow all right?" asked Beatrice.

Ramsay threw his hands up in the air. "That remains to be seen. I thought she was going to blow a gasket when I was flinging baby stuff in the box. She likes things done a particular way you know. But yeah—her ankle is swollen up like crazy. It's got to be a break."

"Do you need me to do anything? I'm calling the vet to reschedule the appointment for Boris, but I can do other things, too."

Ramsay gave her a blank look when she mentioned Boris's appointment . . . the dog's vet visit apparently wasn't on his radar at all. "Uh, no, thanks. Just watch the baby for us and call Piper to let her know you're watching him instead of Meadow. Thanks."

And he dashed away again.

Beatrice would ordinarily have expected Miss Sissy to have pounced on Ramsay to ask him if he'd found her quilt yet, but the old woman was so entranced with the baby that there was no way she was going to think about anything else.

And so a quiet hour was spent. Will was delighted to play with not only his own toys that Ramsay had hastily tossed in the box for him, but the special toys Beatrice kept at her house to entertain her grandson when he visited.

Then Miss Sissy brought out some pots and pans and a metal spoon for Will and herself and the two of them made a tremendous racket with great delight. Beatrice herself was delighted by their total joy for the first few minutes, taking photos and video of the duo. Then, however, she started missing the quiet of her cottage and started thinking about ways they might all be happily quiet together. Despite the noise threatening to curtail her ability to think entirely, Beatrice quickly devised a plan.

"I know," said Beatrice brightly in a voice designed to cut through the racket, "let's go to the Patchwork Cottage."

Miss Sissy gave her a suspicious look as if Beatrice were trying to find a way to put a stop to her and Will's fun. Which, of course, she was. "Why?"

"Well, I'd like to check in with Posy." This was a complete fiction since she'd already seen Posy and gotten her quilting materials. "But mainly because I love seeing Will with Maisie."

Miss Sissy's eyes sparkled and Beatrice saw with relief that she thought this was a brilliant idea. Maisie was partly Miss Sissy's cat and she was likely ready for some time with the feline, herself.

So Beatrice hurried them all out to the driveway and Will into his car seat that lived in the backseat of her car. They drove off to the quilting shop.

Posy gave her a surprised wave and then a knowing look as she spotted Miss Sissy and Will. "Looking for something to do?" she asked, a twinkle in her eye.

"We thought Maisie might need a visit," said Beatrice.

Beatrice realized this couldn't be further from the truth when she spotted the cat happily snoozing in a sunbeam. "Poor Maisie," she chuckled as Will and Miss Sissy toddled toward her. "She was so peaceful."

Posy smiled as Will carefully petted Maisie. "He's so good with her. Always so gentle."

"Well, we had to train him early on how to be sweet with animals. There are so many of them around, after all. I hope it's all right if we kill some time in here. There was drama earlier."

Posy's brow crinkled with alarm and Beatrice added hurriedly, "Nothing too grim. Meadow somehow sprained or broke her ankle. Ramsay thought it was broken. So they brought Will to me and Miss Sissy played with him while I called the vet and rearranged Boris's vet appointment. Then Will and Miss Sissy became extremely loud and I decided a distraction was in order."

The bell on the front door dinged and a very thin, frowsy woman hurried in with hair nearly as messy as Miss Sissy's and an eager, anxious smile. "Good morning! Goodness, I mean 'good afternoon.' Where is my head today? Hi, Posy."

Posy beamed at her. "Hi there, Tiggy! How are you doing today?"

"Oh, pretty well, pretty well. I've been so busy, though, you know? I've got cooking to do for Savannah and I'm working on two dresses for the girls." She smiled happily back at Posy.

Beatrice realized this must be the Aunt Tiggy that Savannah had expressly come over to tell Beatrice about. The one with the healthy, horrid cooking and the dubious dressmaking. But she couldn't help but feel a pang for this rather awkward-looking, earnest, clearly very sweet woman.

Posy quickly said, "Have you met Beatrice yet? Beatrice is another of the Village Quilters."

Tiggy thrust her hand out and gave Beatrice's a hearty shake. "Beatrice! I've heard so many great things about you from the girls. You've been quite a wonderful influence on them, you know."

"Have I?" asked Beatrice, surprised.

"Most definitely so. They're always talking about how level-headed you are and how great you are in a crisis and that sort of thing. It's so nice to know that, when I'm not in town, they have such a fantastic support network. What a comfort."

"Can I help you find anything in the shop today, Tiggy? Or are you here to visit?" asked Posy.

"Like I am," said Beatrice dryly. To Tiggy she said, "My grandson needed a distraction and Maisie the Shop Cat is providing it."

Tiggy gave a happy gasp and put her hand to her throat. "Is the baby here? May I see him?"

"He's right over there with Miss Sissy and Maisie," said Beatrice.

"Is he very shy? I won't scare him, will I?" asked Tiggy tentatively.

"Not a bit. He loves meeting new people."

Tiggy happily scurried over to see the baby as Miss Sissy predictably started scowling at her arrival. The old woman didn't want anyone to get in between her and Will.

Posy said in a low voice while Tiggy cooed over the baby, "I understand from Georgia that Tiggy is very well-intentioned, but is driving them a little crazy."

"She seems really sweet," said Beatrice. "But I did hear she's no fan of junk food. Poor Savannah had to come by and get her fix at my house."

Posy smiled. "She's making clothes for Savannah and Georgia. Matching dresses."

"Oh dear." Savannah and Georgia weren't twins. Even if they were, having matching outfits when you were in your thirties surely wasn't what they'd want.

Posy and Beatrice chatted for a few minutes as Beatrice watched Miss Sissy and Tiggy play with Will and Maisie. Then Tiggy came back over, a frown on her face.

"Is Miss Sissy all right?" she asked with concern.

Beatrice raised her eyebrows. "Well, that's something of a leading question. In what way?"

"I mean, she just seems so *thin*. I can't help but wonder if she's getting all the nutrients she needs."

Posy winked at Beatrice. Beatrice had the feeling that Miss Sissy was going to suddenly find herself with deliveries of tasteless, healthy food.

Beatrice said mildly, "Well, she mostly makes meals for herself but Meadow Downey also brings food over to her several times a week. She's a fabulous cook. She makes a huge helping of whatever she's cooking and then brings it to Miss Sissy and also to my daughter's house since she and her husband are so busy."

"That's very kind of her," said Tiggy. She was thoughtful for a moment. "I wonder if she'd think it was intrusive if I also brought some food over. Maybe some side dishes or lunches."

"You're asking if Miss Sissy would think it was intrusive?"

"No, I mean Meadow. I wouldn't want to make her upset. I was just thinking of ways to help," said Tiggy.

"I'm sure Meadow wouldn't think a thing about it," said Beatrice. "Meadow actually just injured herself so might not even be able to cook for a while. But I'd probably clear it with Miss Sissy first. She can be difficult sometimes, you know."

They looked over at Miss Sissy and, as if on cue, the old woman started snarling at them.

"Yes, I suppose that would be a good idea," said Tiggy slowly.

She strolled back over to tentatively speak with Miss Sissy as the old woman watched her suspiciously. Apparently, Miss Sissy must have growled her approval of the plan because Tiggy came back to them, beaming, as if the old woman had been doing *her* a favor instead of the other way around.

"All set," she said, her face flushed. "Maybe we can get her a little meat on her bones during the time I'm here."

"Are you going to be able to make the guild meeting tomorrow?" asked Posy. "We don't have a speaker this time unfortunately, but we always manage to have fun."

Tiggy sighed. "Oh, I would like to, you know, but I'm afraid I'm going to be busy. I wanted to finish up these dresses I'm making for the girls so that I can see them wear them before I have to head back home. And I'm sure a lot of the business will have to do with the fair, won't it?"

Beatrice said, "Actually, I think almost everything is in place for our part in the fair, although it will be mentioned, of course."

There was the sound of off-key whistling approaching and Dan Whitner appeared in a paint-spattered pair of overalls over a long-sleeved white shirt.

Apparently, Tiggy thought Dan's appearance warranted some tidying up on her end and she hastily smoothed down her wayward hair. Her entire expression transformed into a beaming smile. Beatrice blinked in surprise. Dan was hardly a Lothario, but Tiggy seemed to think he qualified.

Dan said, "All right, Miss Posy, the plumbing in the restroom is all taken care of. I'll go ahead and see about painting the rest of this wall before taking my lunch break."

"Oh, thanks so much, Dan. That leak in there was about to drive me nutty. And it's expensive to have a leak, too. I really appreciate it."

Tiggy eagerly positioned herself closer to Dan. "Goodness, but you're helpful. You can do plumbing *and* painting?"

Dan's eyes opened wider at the praise. A look of pride flashed over his features. "That's right. I guess I can do most oddjobs. Install light fixtures, repair busted drywall, help with siding and roof repairs. I can even maintain heating and air so you don't have to get the HVAC company out."

"That's extraordinarily helpful," said Tiggy rather breathlessly.

Dan straightened a bit. "I can do small stuff, too, like hang pictures or clean grout." He stuck out his hand. "Dan Whitner."

"Tiggy," said Tiggy, not bothering with a last name. "That's amazing. I wish I were good at doing so many things."

Beatrice hid a smile. From what she'd heard from Savannah, Tiggy was definitely someone who *tried* to do a variety of things. But whether she was successful at them was a matter of opinion.

"Got any work that needs to be done?" he asked, still holding on to her hand.

Tiggy giggled. "Oh, not right now. No, I'm visiting with my niece. But I'll be sure to mention to her that you're available if there's anything she needs to get fixed."

The bell on the door suddenly rang and Dan dropped Tiggy's hand as if it was a hot potato.

"Bertha," he gasped, his pale features quickly infused with color.

Chapter Eight

Bertha Cooke was a round woman with shoulder-length curly brown hair and a direct gaze. That direct gaze was now trained on Dan and Tiggy. Tiggy gave her an uncertain smile.

"Ready for lunch, Dan?" asked Bertha.

Dan's brow wrinkled in confusion. "Now? I thought you were doing some cleaning for the Vanderwits."

"They had to reschedule me because Mrs. Vanderwit suddenly had to host bridge. Thought we could go to lunch early."

Posy cleared her throat. "Dan, feel free to go ahead and take your lunch since Bertha is here. You can paint that wall later on."

Tiggy had shrunk away and was now looking through some of Posy's more vibrant fabrics.

Dan frowned. "I ain't hungry yet, Bertha. Just finally finished eating the last of my breakfast not long ago. You go ahead without me."

"I can wait." And instead of leaving to have a solo lunch, Bertha walked over to the sitting area and plopped down next to Miss Sissy, who gave her a cold look and immediately pulled Will out of Bertha's reach.

Bertha, however, didn't seem to have any designs on the baby, instead picking up a fashion magazine and idly flipping through it.

While Posy and Dan were talking about further touch-up work that needed to be done at the Patchwork Cottage, Beatrice walked over to sit across from Bertha.

Bertha glanced up and gave Beatrice a smile and a bob of her head. She did a good deal of cleaning work at the church whenever they needed extra help and she'd always been friendly with Beatrice.

"How're things at the church?" Bertha asked her offhandedly, setting down the magazine.

Miss Sissy looked relieved that Bertha didn't want to play with the baby. Just to be on the safe side, though, she picked up Will and they followed Maisie over near Posy.

"Oh, it's going pretty well. We appreciated your helping out with cleaning up after last weekend's wedding."

Bertha chuckled. "That was a doozy! I don't know how everyone managed to make such a mess. Kinda expected the church hall to be messy after the wedding reception, but the *sanctuary*? There were programs all over the place."

"We were lucky to be able to hire you, from what I understand. I hear you're really in demand as a housekeeper."

Bertha puffed up a bit. "Well, thanks for that. It's pretty true, I have to admit. People don't want to clean up their own messes anymore, so they want to hire somebody on to take care of it for them. I'm just glad it's what I'm good at and there's lots of demand."

Beatrice said slowly, "I believe someone told me you also did work for Linton Hoover."

"I cleaned for him, sure enough. Was going to head over there this morning to do my usual work when the cops told me what happened. They *sort of* told me what happened, anyway. Couldn't get a lot of information from them, even though I was an employee!" Bertha looked miffed. Then she added, "I know you're friends with Meadow. You heard anything about if Ramsay has a lead?"

Beatrice shook her head. "I haven't heard anything to indicate that the police are close to making an arrest."

Bertha snorted. "It's bad when a body can't even feel safe in a small town like Dappled Hills. What's the world coming to?"

"Since you knew Linton, do you have any ideas about what might have happened to him?"

Bertha's eyebrows rose. "What, like if somebody he knew did him in? Why . . . do you think that's what happened?"

"I don't know. But I know I've read that most murders are committed by people the victims know."

Bertha squinched up her face in deep thought for a few moments. Then, in satisfaction, she offered, "Well, there's that Sandra. Can't remember what her last name is. I never really liked her much—she always acts real snobby around me." Bertha sat up straighter, her features flushed with righteous indignation. "I'm doing honest work, you know. And I do a good job! People shouldn't act like they're better than I am."

"I'm sorry she behaved like that around you," said Beatrice softly.

Bertha gave her a mollified look. "Thanks. Anyway, Sandra had a big argument with Mr. Hoover while I was cleaning for him last week. You'd think a person would try to keep their voice down so others wouldn't hear, but like I said, she acted like I wasn't even there. Like I wasn't even worth her attention."

"Did you hear what the argument was about?"

Bertha snorted again. "Sure did—every blessed word until I started vacuuming. I could even hear some of it over the vacuum . . . that's how loud she was screaming at him. You see, she's been mad that Mr. Hoover was seeing somebody else. I guess she thought of Mr. Hoover as her property or something. That would fit right in with her personality. Anyway, she was telling him he had to stop seeing Helen or whatever her name was."

"Heidi?" asked Beatrice.

Bertha pointed a stubby finger at her. "Got it in one. Mr. Hoover didn't want to stop seeing her. Didn't see how it was any of her business that she got to tell him who he could and couldn't date."

"How did Sandra take that?"

Bertha laughed. "Not good at all! She started really yelling at him then. She broke something, too—one of his glass art things. Smashed it all to bits and I had to clean it up after she left. I tell you, some people have no respect at all for others."

"What happened then?"

"She left. Slammed the door behind her and took off real loud in that car of hers, tires screeching and everything. Mr. Hoover looked glad she was gone. My money is on her for killing him." Bertha sniffed.

"So Linton continued seeing Heidi," said Beatrice.

"Yes! And her husband was supposed to be his friend, I hear. Or he was when they were younger. Some friend he is, having an affair with his friend's wife. You'd think that he'd have more respect for their friendship," said Bertha, rather viciously.

"I didn't realize they were friends."

"They grew up together, didn't they? Went to school together, played ball together, that kind of thing."

Beatrice asked, "Are they still that close? Have you seen Aiden over there?"

Bertha gave a caustic laugh. "Not with him knowing his wife is having an affair with him. Which I reckon he knows. Besides, Aiden doesn't have time to be a friend, what with the farm and all. He's got to see after his crops and animals. He doesn't even have time to see after his wife, does he?"

Bertha sat silently for a moment, shaking her head. But Beatrice noticed there was something of a gleeful glint in her eye, possibly at the downfall of her employer.

"What did you think of Linton?" asked Beatrice.

"*Think* of him? Well, I don't have a whole lot of free time to spare a thought for the people who hire me. I'm too busy cleaning up for them. But I can tell you this—Mr. Hoover didn't have as much money as he was saying he did."

"Did he have a lot of debt?" asked Beatrice. "I know he must have put a lot of money into his new house."

"Spent money like there was no tomorrow," said Bertha with a sniff. "And he wasn't all that prompt about paying me. Made me so mad. I was thinking about dropping him as a client. Oh, he'd say he was going to pay me and then the next thing I know, he had to run out of the house suddenly to do an errand. He'd holler behind him that he'd pay me twice the next time. It was really annoying."

"And you think it was because he didn't have the money?" asked Beatrice.

"Naturally. I can tell you he had a bunch of phone calls from debt collectors, too. For cars and what-not. Not that Mr. Hoover would even pick up his phone. He'd let the answering machine pick up."

Beatrice raised her eyebrows in surprise. "A young man like that? I wouldn't think he'd have a landline phone and an answering machine."

"I reckon he didn't want those calls coming to his cell phone. That was his personal phone and he didn't give out the number because maybe he *knew* he'd be getting debt collector calls. So the answering machine would pick up and I could hear the messages clear as day."

"You'd think he wouldn't want you to overhear that." Beatrice frowned.

Bertha shrugged. "Like I said, people act like I'm not even there. I'm kinda invisible, like a ghost or something. But I know a lot about the people I work for because they go on with their private lives right in front of me."

"So you thought he was not as wealthy as he appeared?"

"Not even close! I bet I have more money in my savings account at Dappled Hills Savings and Loan than Mr. Hoover did. The thing that really got on my nerves was that he kept shopping. Oh, the packages that came in! I'd help to unpack them and then I'd have to break the boxes down on my cleaning days. You'd think he'd at least set aside enough money to pay his housekeeper, but that wasn't what was important to him, no sir-ree."

Beatrice asked, "Was he good to work for? Aside from not being prompt with paying you?"

Bertha tilted her head to one side, considering. "Wellll . . . I suppose so. He was right cheerful a lot of the time, even though he had those money problems. And women problems. And problems with his family, too. I reckon he didn't really have that much to be cheerful about, but he tried to be."

"Family problems, too?"

"Oh, yeah. He and his brother did not get along at *all*. I was cleaning one day when that Brett came over. As soon as Mr. Hoover opened the door and saw his brother standing there, he tried to close the door right back again. But Brett put his foot in the door and forced it open while Mr. Hoover was shoving at it from the other side. I thought for a minute that Brett was going to get his foot slammed in the door."

"That's terrible," said Beatrice. "It must be really stressful to not get along with such a close relative."

Bertha shrugged. "I guess so. I don't have family, myself. Brett managed to get in and then started fussing at Mr. Hoover about gambling."

Beatrice said, "Gambling, too?" It was becoming less of a surprise to Beatrice that Linton Hoover had such bad financial problems.

Bertha nodded. "That's what he said, all right. Heard it clear as day. And Mr. Hoover didn't say he *wasn't* gambling, neither. So you asked me what I thought of him. He was really like a big, immature kid who wanted it all. He wanted a big life. Him and his games room and whatnot." Bertha rolled her eyes.

Dan called out, "Bertha? You ready to head out to lunch?"

"You said you weren't hungry," reminded Bertha.

"I might be a little hungrier now. I could eat some fries or something."

"Real healthy," said Bertha, rolling her eyes once more. "Okay, let's head out."

Posy was checking out Tiggy's purchases at the cash register and Beatrice thought Bertha made a real show of being sweet to Dan in front of her. "My beau," said Bertha lovingly to Dan and gave him a peck on the cheek.

Dan blinked with surprise as they headed out the door, the bell ringing behind them as they left.

Tiggy looked wistfully at the door. "I really did like Dan. Are he and Bertha serious?"

Posy gave her a helpless look. "I don't know, Tiggy. They seem like they might be. Dan had mentioned that they'd been going out for a while. I don't know exactly how long, though."

Tiggy sighed. "I've been single my whole life. And just when I thought I might have met a nice, hard-working man, he's taken."

Beatrice said, "Are you planning on staying in Dappled Hills for a while?"

Tiggy gave a short laugh, "Well, I'd definitely consider relocating if I found a good man to spend my life with."

Posy's face brightened as she got an idea. "Oh, I know! Why don't you stay in town a little longer and go to the fair this Saturday? Don't you think that's a good idea, Beatrice?"

Beatrice smiled. She doubted that Savannah and Georgia would think it was such a wonderful idea, but it probably would be good for Tiggy. "That's a great idea, Posy. The fairs are always fun and there are folks there from all around. It would give you the opportunity to meet some people."

"That's really what I need," said Tiggy slowly. "I just need the chance to meet some different people. I live in a small town and there's no real way for me to meet anyone new. At church, everyone is paired up already like the animals on the ark." She paused, thinking this through for a moment. Then she bobbed her head decisively. "That's it. I'll stay."

Posy beamed at her. "That's wonderful."

Tiggy gathered up her purchases and said, "Thanks for the encouragement! That's just what I needed." She looked excited as she said goodbye and left the shop.

Beatrice said, "I should probably be leaving, too. Thanks for providing entertainment for Will and Miss Sissy."

Posy laughed. "I think that was more of Maisie's doing. I hope Meadow will be all right. Have you gotten any texts from Ramsay?"

"Not yet, but I can't imagine he'll be much longer."

Posy said in a low voice, "I don't want to get Miss Sissy riled up again, but did she mention finding her quilt? I'm sure she told you there was one missing."

"She did tell me about it, but she hasn't found it. She's sure that Linton Hoover took it. If he did, Ramsay will get to the bottom of it."

Posy said, "Miss Sissy was telling me about it on the phone yesterday afternoon. She was convinced that it was stolen. I'll admit that part of me wondered if she just couldn't find it in all the clutter. You do think someone stole it?"

Beatrice nodded. "I wondered that myself, but after hearing her describe the quilt, it's certainly valuable if it's in good condition. And all of Miss Sissy's quilts are—she treats them better than she treats anything else in her house."

After a couple more minutes of chatting, Beatrice called back, "Miss Sissy? Will? Are you ready to head back to the house?"

Miss Sissy had a belligerent look on her face. "Time for a snack."

"Well, there really aren't any snacks here at Posy's. We should go back home and find some there."

Posy said, "Goodness, I forgot to bring cookies to the store this morning. I did bake a batch, but didn't put them in the car."

Miss Sissy glowered at Posy as if it were incomprehensible that someone could forget fresh cookies.

Beatrice tried again, "Like I said, we'll get some food at the house, Miss Sissy. I just went to the store, so there is lots of food there."

Miss Sissy muttered something under her breath and Beatrice said, "I couldn't quite make that out, Miss Sissy."

Miss Sissy glowered again, this time pointed at Beatrice. "Yucky food!" she bellowed, as if Beatrice were hard of hearing.

Posy said, "Now, now, Miss Sissy, Beatrice doesn't have bad food in her house. She always has such good things there."

"Not now!" insisted Miss Sissy.

Beatrice sighed. "Actually, Posy, in Miss Sissy's opinion, the food probably *isn't* very good. Wyatt's starting a 'whole foods' diet and I went to the store to bring in a bunch of fruits and vegetables. Apparently, they're not exactly what Miss Sissy is looking for today. Even though I know she eats plenty of healthy foods at home."

Miss Sissy gave her a baleful look. Apparently, when she was visiting others, she didn't want to have anything remotely healthy.

Posy said, "I've got an unopened bag of chips in the back from one of the last guild meetings. You could take that...Cork and I have lots of chips at home."

Miss Sissy looked wistfully at Posy as if hoping for an invitation to *her* house, instead.

But Beatrice fetched the chips and then herded the old woman and Will into the car. Sadly, not only did Will become fussy on the way back to the house, but Miss Sissy did, too. Beatrice had already thought Miss Sissy a little cranky, but that was nothing compared to her current mood. Naps looked as if they might be in everyone's future. Otherwise, Ramsay and Meadow were going to end up with a very grouchy baby on their hands.

Chapter Nine

Once they got inside, Beatrice took Noo-noo out to potty and Miss Sissy opened up the bag of chips. Will wasn't much of a fan and continued fussing, sticking a chubby finger in his mouth. Beatrice pulled some grapes out and cut each one into a million different pieces. There would be no choking babies on her watch. She smiled as Will took handfuls and stuffed them into his mouth.

There was a knock at the door and Noo-noo erupted into happy barking, anticipating that someone she liked was at the door. Sure enough, it was Ramsay. A tired-looking Ramsay.

"How is Meadow?" asked Beatrice.

Ramsay rubbed his forehead. "Well, she's broken that ankle, as we thought. She's going to have to stay off of it for a while to let it heal. Of course, Meadow being Meadow, that's going to practically be impossible."

Beatrice said slowly, "There's no way she can watch the baby, then. Especially with you investigating a murder."

Ramsay nodded. "That's exactly what I was going to tell you. She was trying to convince me that she absolutely *could* watch Will. Who knows—maybe she can figure out a way for tomorrow, but for the rest of the day I think she needs to put her feet up. Do you mind watching Will for the rest of the afternoon?"

"Not a bit," said Beatrice. "In fact, I was just getting ready to put him down for a nap." She lowered her voice, "And Miss Sissy, too."

Ramsay chuckled and then stepped inside the house for a moment as Miss Sissy strode up to them.

"Something I can help you with, Miss Sissy?" asked Ramsay respectfully.

"Where's my quilt?"

Ramsay snapped his fingers. "Actually, I was going to come by and talk to you about that later today. We *did* find your quilt. At least, we assume it's your quilt."

Miss Sissy looked increasingly agitated and Beatrice said, "Let me help with identifying it. Miss Sissy described the quilt at length to me earlier."

Ramsay took out his notebook and Beatrice described the quilt with Miss Sissy interjecting from time-to-time to add salient details. Then he nodded decisively, closed his notebook, and put it away. "Miss Sissy, that's definitely your quilt."

"Want it back," said the old woman in a sullen voice.

"And you most certainly will get it back. Probably tomorrow, but don't you worry, it's coming back to you."

"Found it in *his* house?"

"In a closet. And I can promise you, having gone through his house with a fine-tooth comb, it's not the sort of item that would have coordinated with the rest of his furnishings and decorations. I can only imagine that he was planning on selling it," said Ramsay.

Beatrice cleared her throat. "Actually, I might be able to help with that a little. I'm supposing the quilt was in good condition?"

"Well, I don't know a lot about quilts, but there weren't any holes in it or mildew on it or anything like that."

Miss Sissy glared at Beatrice.

"Sorry," said Beatrice, "I know you take good care of your things. I was just trying to think about the quilt in terms of an appraiser. Considering the age of it and its good condition, a collector might pay as much as five thousand dollars for it."

Ramsay grunted. "Well, then. Yeah, he was going to sell it. I just don't know how the guy realized its value."

"He seemed to have a good eye for valuable things, from what I've heard. And I'm sure you and the state police are coming to the same conclusion, but Linton appeared to have some financial problems. I spoke with Bertha Cooke today and she mentioned Linton was a gambler."

"Wicked!" opined Miss Sissy.

Ramsay's eyebrows flew up. "Did she, now? Well, that's a very interesting bit of information. We've been able to get into his banking a little bit so far. I can't disclose much, but our findings seem to reflect that Linton might not have been opposed to trying to make some extra money. I take it his expenses had been very steep with the construction and furnishing of his house. What else did you find out today?"

Ramsay took the notebook back out as Beatrice talked about Linton and his brother's difficult relationship, Heidi's devotion for Linton, and Sandra's anger at being displaced as Linton's girlfriend. She was careful not to mention any information that Heidi had personally given her, instead giving Ramsay what she'd heard about Heidi and Sandra from other sources.

Miss Sissy listened with satisfaction. "It wasn't me!"

Ramsay said, "Miss Sissy, I never said you had a thing to do with Linton's death. There seem to be plenty of people he upset. But you know I have to do my job and talk to everybody who had a problem with Linton, and that does include you. It doesn't mean I believe you killed him."

His answer seemed to placate Miss Sissy a little. Then he added sternly, "But I wanted to speak with you about one important thing. Locking your door."

Miss Sissy looked down at the floor.

"It's clear to me that Linton must have just walked into your house, spotted that quilt, and walked right back out again with it. If your door had been locked, I'm sure he wouldn't have stolen that quilt."

"Thief!" Miss Sissy hissed.

"Yes. Yes, he apparently was a thief. But I doubt he would have wanted a charge of breaking and entering. It sounds like he was just underwater with debt, feeling desperate, and probably figured you'd never even realize the quilt was missing," said Ramsay.

Miss Sissy, wanting to escape the lecture, stomped off to play with Will who was pushing around a toy truck.

Ramsay turned to Beatrice, "I'd be interested in hearing what your impressions were after listening to all that today."

Beatrice took a deep breath. "Well, I didn't have a great impression of Linton Hoover before, but he definitely went down in my esteem after listening to everyone talk about him. He seemed to be on everyone's bad side. He was a bad neighbor, a bad boyfriend, a bad brother. And apparently, he wasn't very careful with his money, so he was bad with his personal finances."

Ramsay frowned. "If Linton was secretly seeing Heidi Wheeler, I have to wonder what Aiden thinks about that. Was that something he knew about?"

"I haven't spoken to him, but I'll likely be visiting his roadside stand tomorrow to get some fresh tomatoes."

Ramsay's frown deepened. "Now Beatrice, I don't need you getting any more involved in this than you already are."

"Oh, I know. It's just that Wyatt is trying to eat more healthily and I thought some local tomatoes might help with that. The ones they have at the store aren't quite as good as Aiden's. Maybe I'll pick up something while I'm there. You never know—maybe even just an impression. Sometimes people confide in me."

Ramsay gave her a wry look. "That must be nice. People *don't* tend to confide in me. I wonder why."

Beatrice chuckled. "Well, that's more to do with your job than it is with you. Are you still thinking about retirement?"

"Thinking about it, yes. But I'm just not sure if I can quite pull it off yet." He sighed.

"You'd be able to get a lot more writing done," said Beatrice. She was careful not to mention the award Ramsay had won that she wasn't supposed to know about.

Ramsay's expression brightened. "That's very true. Oh, I fit in a good amount of short story writing on a *normal* day. But when there's an investigation going on, that's completely impossible. I'll enjoy getting back to it and getting back to my reading again, too." He quirked an eyebrow. "How's the book I lent you?"

"You mean *As I Lay Dying*?" Ramsay was in the habit of lending Beatrice his favorite books for her to read. But William Faulkner wasn't exactly something you could speed-read. "I'm making a little progress, but it's been slow going."

Ramsay said, "Well, as soon as you finish that one, I have another Faulkner gem for you. Maybe it won't be good right now with everything going on, but *The Sound and the Fury* is an excellent read. It just might be a little dark."

Beatrice snorted. "*As I Lay Dying* isn't exactly a *light* read, Ramsay. It starts out with a dying mother watching her son construct her coffin."

"Ah, right. But it's such an interesting book, isn't it?"

"It's extraordinarily well-written," admitted Beatrice. "It's just that I have to have my A-game on when I'm reading it. It's not the sort of book you can skim. And there are so many characters to keep up with. I had to make myself a cheat-sheet."

Ramsay was about to respond to this when his phone rang. He peered at it and sighed. "Meadow."

He answered his phone and said, "How's everything at the house? Have you settled in?"

Meadow spoke on the other end for a couple of minutes. Beatrice couldn't make out the words, but she could tell Meadow was very animated.

Ramsay frowned. "Now, Meadow, we talked about this. There's no way you can take care of Will with a broken ankle. Beatrice is happy to look after him. In fact, she's about to put him down for a nap."

He rolled his eyes at Beatrice and she gave him a sympathetic look.

Meadow gave a long monologue before Ramsay finally interjected, "What about picking him up to put him in his high chair?"

Meadow apparently had an answer for that.

"What about putting him in his crib?" demanded Ramsay.

There was another answer for that.

"And in his car seat? You can't even drive right now!" said Ramsay.

And yet Meadow seemed to have a response for that, too.

Ramsay grumbled, "All right. We'll give it a go. But if you run into any problems, call Beatrice."

He glanced at Beatrice to make sure that was all right and she nodded.

He hung up with Meadow and gave a tremendous sigh. "She's just not wanting to give up her time with that baby."

Beatrice asked curiously, "How did she say she was going to handle it all? The high chair, crib, etc?"

Ramsay rubbed his eyes and laughed shortly. "Oh, she has a plan for everything. She's put out a few beach blankets on the kitchen floor for Will to eat there. And she's made up a little bed for him on the floor in our bedroom."

Beatrice frowned. "What about Boris?"

"You know how that huge animal loves Will. Meadow thinks Boris won't even try to eat Will's food because it's *Will*." Ramsay shrugged.

"But it's Boris. Boris has eaten things off my countertops before." It was hard for Beatrice to imagine Boris being well-behaved around food. But she supposed stranger things had happened.

"And the car seat? The driving?" asked Beatrice.

Ramsay said, "And there's the rub. She acknowledges that she won't be able to go anywhere with the baby. So it's going to be Camp Meadow at our house. Fortunately, she has lots of ideas for activities."

"I can only imagine," said Beatrice dryly. Meadow did put a lot of time and energy into entertaining their grandson.

Ramsay scooped up Will, earning a dirty look from Miss Sissy as Beatrice started putting Will's toys and baby equipment back into the box they arrived in. A minute later, Ramsay and Will were getting in the car.

Miss Sissy, her source of entertainment stolen from her, stood up and headed grumpily for the door to make her own exit from Beatrice's suddenly less interesting house that had no good snacks.

"At least Ramsay found your quilt," offered Beatrice.

Miss Sissy gave an unimpressed harumph and took her leave.

Beatrice tidied up for a few minutes and then turned to Noo-noo, who was looking at her expectantly. "It's nice to have some quiet, isn't it, girl? Let's go in the backyard."

With Noo-noo trotting happily behind her, Beatrice picked up her book and headed for the hammock. Usually the little dog wanted to lie on the ground beside her, but this time she looked pointedly up at the hammock.

"You want to get up there?" asked Beatrice doubtfully. "But your little legs will fall through the hammock's netting. Here, let me get a quilt."

She got a quilt from inside, spreading it carefully over the bottom of the hammock before collecting the corgi and climbing in with her.

Noo-noo fell asleep right away, giving puffy little snores. Beatrice tried to focus on her book. But, as she'd told Ramsay, Faulkner's *As I Lay Dying* did require quite a bit of concentration. There were plenty of characters to keep up with. As she tried to sort out exactly what was going on with the story, she felt her eyelids getting heavier. It didn't help that the little dog beside her seemed to be coaching her into napping.

When she woke up, the sun was going down and Wyatt was looking down at her sympathetically. "Big day?" he asked.

She filled him in on the rest of it: Meadow's ankle, Will and Miss Sissy, and their time at the Patchwork Cottage.

"No wonder you fell asleep. You must be completely exhausted," he said. He glanced at her book. "Of course, reading Faulkner didn't help, I'm sure."

Beatrice chuckled. "Well, it's a very well-written book."

"Considering who wrote it, I'm sure that's the case."

"It just requires a little more focus than I can give it today," admitted Beatrice.

They walked inside and Wyatt fed Noo-noo her supper. Then he opened up the fridge and then the cabinets. He turned, giving Beatrice a warm smile. "You went to the store for me. You didn't have to do that." He paused and added, "I'm not even sure *when* you did that, with the day you just described to me."

She gave him a wry look. "Well, I *bought* the food. Clearly, I haven't prepared anything. Frankly, I'm not really sure what to do with some of it, so I hoped you had some ideas. Maybe we could steam some of the vegetables? And just eat the fruit raw?"

Wyatt glanced at the different healthy options. "Yes, I think that sounds good. Or maybe I should roast the vegetables, since I could do a whole sheet pan that way. I'll just put some olive oil and sea salt on them."

"I'll help chop up the veggies," said Beatrice, moving into the kitchen.

Wyatt gently stopped her. "You've had a busy enough day. Why don't you sit in the living room and put your feet up for a while? Read your book."

Beatrice snorted. "You saw what happened earlier when I tried to read my book."

"Work on your quilt, then. Or do whatever you can think of to relax. I've got this, I promise. I don't want to create any extra work for you simply because I need to go on a diet."

Beatrice didn't have to be told again. Cooking had never been her favorite chore, and now she was in somewhat unfamiliar territory with the healthy, raw foods. Her usual modus operandi was to create a vegetable casserole . . . possibly with a can of cream-of-something soup in it. But she had the feeling that the soup would most definitely be considered a no-no for a whole-foods diet.

She'd just kicked off her shoes and was stretched out on their comfy sofa when her phone rang insistently. Beatrice groaned.

"You don't have to get that, you know," said Wyatt.

But Beatrice had already picked up. And then she immediately regretted it. Dora Tucker, a volunteer at the church, fellow quilter, and all-round community-minded resident was on the line. And when Dora called her, she usually had a task for Beatrice.

Dora said briskly in that no-nonsense voice of hers, "Beatrice. Hope you're well. Listen, I'm calling about the fair. You're going, I presume."

It really wasn't a question. "Yes, I'll be there," said Beatrice cautiously. She winced. At the last event, she'd served as the clean-up crew with Dora. She'd decided then that she'd rather take on a different role at the next one. Cleaning up after a barrage of fair-goers was not her idea of fun. And surely, there must be a younger volunteer who'd be better-suited to the task.

"Good. I was wondering if the fair could borrow some of the church's audio equipment for our second entertainment stage. We have the first stage covered, but the second one needs some help. Will the equipment be available?"

Beatrice said, "Let me check with Wyatt and find out." She bounced across the room and into the kitchen, pleased that Dora didn't seem to be calling to recruit her for work, after all.

After she'd asked, he said, "I can't think of any conflicts that day. We'd be happy to loan it out."

Beatrice passed this along to Dora, who sounded pleased. "Wonderful. Then that's taken care of." She paused. "I also wanted to see if you were on any of the committees for the fair. We do need some help."

Beatrice closed her eyes momentarily and then opened them to see Wyatt's amused expression. "Not this time, no. Usually,

I'm happy to help out but I wanted to just attend the fair as a grandma this time. I want to see Will on all the baby rides."

Dora's voice now sounded irritated. "I see. Well, if that changes, do let me know. We can use all the hands we can."

Beatrice was about to apologize for her lack of civic initiative, but Dora had already hung up.

"She hung up on me," said Beatrice in dawning outrage.

Wyatt's eyebrows shot up. "Did she really?"

Beatrice said, "She did. She didn't like me turning her down. Dora Tucker is one of those people who always gets her way. She'll probably figure out a way to recruit me at the fair. She'll be dragging me off to help with the craft tents or have me taking tickets." Her face fell, glumly.

Wyatt said, "Well, regardless, I'm very proud of you."

"For not volunteering?"

"For saying no. I know you wanted to spend time with Will at the fair and why wouldn't you? He's at such a great age where everything is new and fun and amazing and you want to experience the event through his eyes. Besides, it's not as if you don't do a lot of volunteer work. It's all right to take a break every now and then," said Wyatt gently.

This made Beatrice feel a bit better. "Thanks. I felt bad about it because I know they need people to help out. But they need to find some *fresh* people to help out. The problem in Dappled Hills is that they always tap the same people to volunteer and we all get burned out."

Beatrice's phone rang again and she looked warily at it. "Surely that's not Dora calling back with a new and improved pitch for getting me to work the fair."

She glanced at her phone and relaxed a little as she saw it was Meadow. Picking up the phone, she said, "Meadow? How are you doing? How's Will?" She worried that Meadow was calling because she needed help with the baby.

Meadow said crisply, "I'm just fine and so is Will! At least, I suppose Will is fine—Piper has already picked him up. Everyone is fussing over me, though, and it's driving me crazy."

Chapter Ten

"**B**y everyone, do you mean Ramsay?" Beatrice grinned.

"Yes, Ramsay's driving me crazy. He doesn't want me to do anything, Beatrice, and it's just so silly. You'd think I had a really serious injury instead of a broken ankle."

"I'd think a broken ankle *would* qualify as a serious injury. You can't put any weight on it, can you? It must make getting around very tricky."

"I've certainly had worse challenges in my life and have been able to surmount them. Ramsay keeps calling in to check. You'd think he didn't have a murder to investigate."

Beatrice said, "I'm sure he's just concerned about you, Meadow. He probably wants to make sure you're resting and not overdoing it."

Meadow said glumly, "No chance of that. I can't seem to be able to cook, which is most annoying."

"No, I suppose you can't. You wouldn't be able to keep the pressure off your foot and use crutches while stirring things on the stove. Would you like Wyatt and me to bring you some food? You've done that so many times for me."

Meadow's voice lost its irritated edge for a minute. "Oh Beatrice, that's so sweet of you. But no—I have so many meals in the freezer and the freezer in the garage. You know how I am about meal prep. We should have enough to eat to last us through my recovery. But I just hate that I can't bring anything to Miss Sissy or Piper and Ash like I was used to."

"I wouldn't worry about Miss Sissy," said Beatrice dryly. "When I was at the Patchwork Cottage earlier today, Tiggy said she was going to do some cooking for her."

"Goodness. I thought Savannah said Tiggy was a terrible cook."

Beatrice said, "Well, I think she's definitely a healthy foods person. We'll see how Miss Sissy adapts to that. And I'm sure I can try and pitch in for Piper and Ash. Wyatt and I are *also* doing a healthy foods diet and we can always make extra."

Meadow sounded more chipper now. "That would be great! Oh, and I did have a big favor to ask you, which I hate to do because I know you're busy."

Beatrice winced in anticipation and Wyatt gave her a sympathetic look. "What is it?"

"Could you take Boris to the vet for me tomorrow? There's no way Ramsay can do it with the investigation and I know I couldn't handle Boris and my crutches. Oh, and thank you for calling them to reschedule the appointment—that was most helpful. It's just that Boris is due for his shots and I don't want his vaccinations to expire, especially with him spending time around the baby."

"Of course I'll help out." Beatrice looked at the ceiling and briefly closed her eyes again as Wyatt hid a grin. "I'll run by and pick him up tomorrow morning."

After she'd hung up, she said to Wyatt, "If the phone rings again, do me a favor and stop me from answering it."

"Are you getting your free time spoken for?" he asked.

"Yes, not that there's much of it," she said with a sigh. "I have to take Boris to the vet for Meadow tomorrow. I'll have to be sure to take my vitamins if I'm to wrestle that gigantic beast."

"I could take him for you," said Wyatt. "That does seem like it would be hard to juggle him while you're signing him in and paying at the end."

Beatrice shook her head firmly. "Now you're volunteering some of *your* rare free time. No, if Meadow can do it, I can do it." She squared her jaw. "And now, on that note, I'm going to retire to the bedroom."

Wyatt glanced at the clock in surprise.

"Don't worry—I'm not falling asleep . . . yet. But I'm going to need to get some rest for my day tomorrow."

Noo-noo trotted after her and minutes later they were curled up on the bed together as Beatrice worked through the convolutions of *As I Lay Dying*.

Despite her best efforts, Beatrice had fallen asleep a bit earlier than she'd planned on. Consequently, she arose before dawn. Noo-noo looked at her in surprise as she got up, stumbled into the kitchen, and made coffee.

"Yes, I know—it's not even light outside," she said to the little dog in her gruff morning voice. She let the corgi out and then fixed her a bowl of kibbles while her coffee perked.

Beatrice never enjoyed getting up before dawn, but she enjoyed *having gotten up* before dawn. She liked all the things she was able to accomplish. She started by mapping out her day on paper since there were several moving parts—a trip to the vet, a visit to Aiden's roadside stand for fresh tomatoes, and the guild meeting. Then she quietly did some tidying up around the cottage, apparently succeeding in her quest not to wake up Wyatt.

When it finally grew light enough, she put on a light jacket and took Noo-noo for a walk. She saw Miss Sissy's lights were on and raised her eyebrows in surprise. She wasn't sure if the old woman always got up this early or if she was just up early today. Continuing down the road, she and Noo-noo came across a deer and they all froze. The look on Noo-noo's face indicated that she believed she'd just seen a very large and strange-looking dog. She finally broke up the tableau by jumping into a paroxysm of barking and the deer bounded off into the woods.

When Beatrice and Noo-noo had turned around and were heading back home, she saw Miss Sissy was now outside. Not only was she outside, actually, she was peering in Linton Hoover's windows.

Beatrice gave a cough and Miss Sissy sprang away from the window, hissing.

"I don't think you should probably be on Linton's property, Miss Sissy. You know that you already look sort of suspicious since you and Linton argued right before he died."

The old woman glared at her. "Didn't do anything to him."

"I know you didn't and Ramsay knows you didn't, but the state police don't know that. And if they were to come by and see you looking in Linton's windows, they might wonder about it."

Miss Sissy's face was sullen. "Want my quilt back."

"And I'm sure you'll get it back," said Beatrice soothingly. "But not yet. And I'm pretty sure it's probably not even inside Linton's house anymore. Since the quilt was reported stolen, it could be that it was taken to the police department."

Miss Sissy grumbled and looked generally out of sorts.

Beatrice asked, "By the way, did Meadow tell you that she wasn't able to cook? She can't handle both her crutches and cooking at the same time. But Tiggy is bringing you food, isn't she?"

Miss Sissy scowled. "Yucky food."

"I believe it was supposed to be healthy food."

The old woman made a face. Beatrice remembered that Savannah complained that Tiggy didn't really season her food.

"Did you eat what she brought you last night?" asked Beatrice.

Miss Sissy nodded but looked as if it hadn't been her first choice.

"If you need anything, just let me know. Wyatt and I cook every night, too and we usually have extra."

"More yucky food," muttered the old woman.

"*Healthy* food," corrected Beatrice with a sigh although part of her was inclined to agree with Miss Sissy. "All right, well, Noo-noo and I should head back home now. I'll see you at the guild meeting."

When she got back to the house, Wyatt was already up and had scrambled some eggs with some onions and peppers. He grinned sleepily at her when she came in.

"Hope I didn't wake you up this morning," said Beatrice. "I was trying to be quiet but it seems like the more I try to be quiet, the louder I become."

He shook his head. "You didn't wake me up at all. How long have you been up?"

"Wayyy too long. I fell asleep far too early last night trying to wrangle with *As I Lay Dying*. But I want to finish it since it's one of Ramsay's favorite books. I might have to look it up online and read some articles on it so I can figure out what direction Faulkner was trying to head in."

They had breakfast together and then Wyatt headed off for the church. Beatrice decided to go ahead and chop vegetables in preparation for supper that night since she knew she was going to have a full day. Glancing at the clock, she figured she'd go ahead and head over to Meadow's to take Boris to the vet. She put a few of Noo-noo's treats in her pocket in case she needed to bribe the big guy in any way.

Meadow greeted her at the door, swinging her hurt foot as she leaned heavily on the crutches. Boris, already in his harness, greeted Beatrice ecstatically.

"He's full of himself this morning," said Meadow, scratching Boris affectionately behind the ears.

"Oh, boy," said Beatrice glumly.

Boris flung himself on the floor for a tummy rub and Beatrice gave him one for at least a minute, hoping it would calm the dog down. He was a sweet boy but full of energy and mischief. He grinned his big grin and she swore he winked at her.

"How are you doing?" asked Beatrice, glancing up at Meadow from the floor.

Meadow made a face. "Just aggravated. It's so annoying to have all these things you want to do and not be able to do them. At least I've figured out how to keep Will here. Piper is going to bring him by soon. Thanks again for doing the vet errand." She paused and added carefully, "Sometimes Boris gets a little sad about going to the vet. The poor boy. I could send you with some treats to help cheer him up."

"I've actually packed some to bring with me, just in case."

Meadow brightened. "A fabulous idea. Beatrice, you're always such a wonderful planner. Really always so extraordinary."

Beatrice got the distinct impression that Meadow might be buttering her up. But she gave her a smile and said, "Now you need to go put that foot up for a while. You're not going to get better unless you rest it."

Meadow heaved a heavy sigh. "I guess. It's just awful, Beatrice, feeling trapped in this house."

"You'll also need a ride to the guild meeting this afternoon, won't you? I know there's no way you're able to drive." Or there *shouldn't* be. And Beatrice was determined not to have an injured Meadow terrorizing the streets of Dappled Hills.

Meadow made a face. "I wasn't all that sure I was going to go. We'll see if I feel up to it."

Now Beatrice stared at Meadow with alarm. "Not go to a guild meeting? You *never* miss guild meetings."

"Well, usually I'm not stumbling around on crutches."

Beatrice tilted her head to one side and carefully observed Meadow. The only reason Meadow could possibly not want to go to a quilt guild meeting, as far as Beatrice could imagine, would be if Meadow felt down in the dumps. "I'll pick up you and Will this afternoon?"

"Will is the one bright spot in my day," said Meadow gloomily.

"The guild meeting will be another," announced Beatrice in a decisive tone. She gave a gentle pull on Boris's leash toward the door and Boris gave a very un-gentle pull in response, eagerly yanking Beatrice across the living room area and to the door, wagging his tail in great excitement.

"See you in a little while," said Meadow. "Good luck at the vet. And thanks."

Beatrice gave Meadow another searching look before Boris lugged her to her car. She managed to wrestle him into her back-seat where she had Noo-noo's seat belt set up for Boris's harness to attach to.

She spoke to Boris as she drove. Beatrice figured a calm voice would soothe the tremendous dog and hopefully get him into a sort of Zen state of mind. "Now, we're going to see your doctor, Boris. They're good people over there and they're want-ing to take care of you and make sure you stay healthy and well. And there will be treats."

Beatrice couldn't see Boris in the rearview because he was so tall on the seat, but she heard him happily panting. A minute later, he scratched at the window and she obediently put it down a notch so he could stick out his massive nose and smell whatev-er wonderful smells were outside as they drove slowly by.

However, as soon as they pulled into the parking lot of the veterinarian's office, there was a big change in Boris's demeanor. Apparently, he smelled something familiar that he actively disliked. He abruptly pulled his head back in the window and seemed to be attempting to hide his gigantic body in a corner of Beatrice's car.

This did not bode well. Beatrice parked the car and got out, opening the back door. "Boris," she called gently. "Hey there. We need to go inside, buddy."

Boris had covered up his eyes with his huge paws. Beatrice suspected his theory was: "If I can't see you, you can't see me." Unfortunately for Boris, he was quite mistaken and he was very visible. In fact, despite the fact he'd made himself as small as possible, he was still taking up most of Beatrice's backseat.

"Let's go, Boris."

Boris gave a whimper.

"It's okay, I promise. Look, I brought treats." Beatrice rummaged around in her pockets and pulled out a treat.

Boris sniffed the air and then briefly removed his paws from his face. He gave the treat a look and then covered his eyes back up.

Beatrice had the distinct impression that Boris was bargaining with her. "Okay, here are a few treats." She pulled a couple more out.

Boris looked again and crept toward her. But before she could grab the leash and try manhandling him out of the car, he slurped up the treats with his tongue and huddled back in his corner.

"Okay. I'm going to have to call for reinforcements," muttered Beatrice. She took out her cell phone and called the front desk. "Hi there, I'm here with Boris Downey for an appointment and he refuses to get out of the car." She gave an awkward laugh. "Could someone come out and give me a hand? I think I'm going to need to have some help."

"We'll be right out," said the chipper voice of the receptionist.

Beatrice hung up and Boris watched her balefully as if knowing what was coming. "This has happened before, hasn't it?" asked Beatrice.

Boris looked down at the seat, not meeting her eyes.

"I think Meadow realizes she had a lucky escape. If breaking an ankle could be considered lucky."

The front door of the vet building opened and the receptionist came out . . . with Sandra. Beatrice blinked. Noo-noo went to this vet too, but she saw a different veterinarian. If Beatrice had realized Sandra was a vet, she'd completely forgotten it. Maybe that's why Sandra had felt so comfortable knocking on Meadow's door the morning Linton died . . . not only was she getting the police chief, she was also going to the house of a patient of hers.

Sandra gave her a smile. "Beatrice? I wasn't expecting to see you here. How did Meadow get you to run this errand for her?"

Beatrice said dryly, "Well, she broke her ankle, I'm afraid, and can't drive. I agreed to help, but didn't realize Boris had a deeply ingrained fear of coming here."

"Oh, he's phobic," agreed Sandra cheerfully. "But don't worry, we're used to it. Once we finally get him inside, he's as right as rain."

Between the receptionist and Sandra, they were able to wrangle and coerce Boris out of the backseat. Finally on the ground, he gave Beatrice a hangdog expression as he was led inside with Beatrice following them.

Sandra gave Boris a quick and thorough examination while the dog sat glumly on the exam table. Beatrice had to admit that Sandra seemed to have a way with the animal, though, and Boris didn't struggle as she looked him over and then administered his vaccines.

Sandra rubbed him and Boris gave her a soulful look. "See, that wasn't so bad," she crooned to him.

"You've got a special way with him," said Beatrice. "I was expecting you to have a really tough time trying to examine him."

They chatted for a minute and then Sandra said in a carefully offhanded manner, "I know you and Meadow spend a good deal of time together. Have you heard anything more about any developments with Linton's murder?"

Beatrice shook her head. "Not as far as I've heard. Although of course they could have some leads and Ramsay is just keeping them under his hat. If he told Meadow, it would be all over Dappled Hills in minutes, you know."

Sandra nodded her head absently. "It's just not right for Linton to be dead and his killer to be running around completely free. He's got to come to justice." She said, almost to herself, "Maybe I can help give them a lead."

Beatrice said, "If you know anything, you should tell the police. Someone who kills once might kill again and you could prevent that."

"Of course. Not that I really know anything, but I'll be sure to reach out. Now, on to Mr. Boris, here."

Sandra gave Beatrice a summary of Boris's health which was that he was all vaccinated, that he was in good health, but that he could stand to lose a pound or two.

Boris wasn't nearly as difficult to herd out of the vet as he had been to wrestle into the building. He pulled Beatrice ahead of him as if she were on roller skates. She managed to checkout at the front desk and then escorted the dog into the car.

"That was absolutely exhausting, Boris," she said sternly to the dog, who grinned at her. "A big boy like you shouldn't be so afraid of going to the doctor."

Boris winked at her.

"All right. Well, we're going to stop by Aiden's roadside stand to get some tomatoes. Do you think you can be good during a short errand?"

Boris grinned again and drooled a bit on Beatrice's backseat.

Chapter Eleven

The farm was out in the country, but the stand that Aiden used to sell his crops to the town was fairly centrally-located in a large parking lot downtown. Fortunately, the lot was deserted. Beatrice took Boris out of the car and they walked up to Aiden. He was a wiry, rangy man, tall and tanned with a quiet dignity about him. He lifted a hand as Beatrice and Boris approached.

"Hi there," he said with a smile. "This isn't your dog, is it? I thought I remembered you had something a little smaller."

"You remember something a *lot* smaller," said Beatrice. "I'm helping out Meadow and Ramsay and this is their dog, Boris. He's very poorly-behaved."

At that point, however, Boris decided to prove Beatrice completely wrong. He politely smiled at Aiden and then rolled over onto his back for a belly rub. After Aiden gave him a gentle rub, Boris rolled back onto his feet again and sat quietly there next to Beatrice.

"Do you mind picking out a few tomatoes for me?" asked Beatrice. "They all look fantastic."

While Aiden was carefully examining the tomatoes and putting a select few into a grocery bag, he said gruffly, "One of my customers said something a little while ago and I wondered if you knew whether it was true or not."

"What did they say?"

Aiden put the tomatoes on the scale. "They said that Linton Hoover had died."

Beatrice nodded. "Yes, and I'm sorry. I know that you grew up together here."

She watched as a strange look of satisfaction crossed Aiden's features. "This might be wrong of me to say, but I can't pretend to be sorry. Linton was my friend, but then he started doing very unfriendly things to hurt me."

"I'm sorry to hear that," said Beatrice softly.

Aiden sighed. "I've been busy working with the cows the last couple of days and I reckon that's why I haven't heard about it. I know news usually travels fast in Dappled Hills."

Beatrice realized that Heidi clearly hadn't mentioned anything about Linton's death to Aiden, but that would hardly be a conversation Heidi would want to initiate.

Aiden told her the price of the tomatoes and Beatrice opened her purse and took out a couple of bills. "The police don't seem to have leads yet. You did hear it wasn't a natural death?"

Aiden nodded, a muscle in his head twitching. "That's what I heard."

"Do you have any idea who might have done something like that?"

Aiden gave a humorless laugh. "Brett, his brother, might have had something to do with it. Those two never did get along—guess they were too different. Even as kids, they were always carping at each other."

"Brothers sometimes do, I guess."

Aiden lifted a brow. "Oh, they do. But this always kind of seemed mean-spirited to me. That's all I know." He came around the stand to see Boris, who was acting like a very good boy and Boris closed his eyes happily as Aiden rubbed his head and scratched him behind his ears.

Beatrice cleared her throat and said, "How is Heidi doing? I haven't seen her at church lately."

A shutter dropped down over Aiden's features. He gave Boris a final pat and then stood back up. "She's doing fine, I guess. Probably just hasn't wanted to make it into town."

Beatrice knew that wasn't right. It sounded as if Heidi had been making it into town a little too often, if anything.

A minute later, Beatrice and Boris were heading back to Meadow's house. Beatrice tapped on the door and could hear Meadow's crutches thumping on the wooden floor as she made her way to the door and opened it.

Boris gave her a huge grin and she threw her arms around the animal, crutches falling to the wayside as she did. Then Boris trotted over to where Will was playing with blocks on the floor and gave the baby a joyful lick on the top of his fluffy hair that made Will giggle.

"How did his appointment go?" asked Meadow in a carefully-casual voice.

Beatrice handed her the crutches back and said rather sternly, "It went fine after three of us managed to wrestle Boris out of the car and into the vet's office."

Meadow had the grace to blush. "Oh, was it tough to get him inside?"

"You could say that. He's not exactly a creature that's easy to move when he doesn't want to move."

Boris had happy zoomies around the barn before flinging himself down on his back and rolling around delightedly as Will giggled at him. "Well, thanks *so* much for running that errand for me. It sure looks like he's in a good mood."

"Boris was a lot more chipper after we left the vet. We stopped by Aiden's roadside stand and picked up tomatoes after that. Boris seemed to like Aiden." Beatrice glanced at her watch. "I'd better head on back home so I can have some time before the guild meeting. Which I'll be picking you up for."

Meadow sighed. "Yes, all right. You've convinced me. It's just going to be a whole lot of bother, though."

"Bother or not, that's the plan. I'll text you before I head over."

Beatrice hurried home, let Noo-noo out and fed her, then put her feet up for a while. She'd set her alarm just in case and it was a good thing she had—it woke her up with a start when it went off. Beatrice jumped up, brushed her teeth and hair and texted Meadow.

Meadow was uncharacteristically cranky. She had a quilt she wanted to bring for the sew-and-tell portion of the meeting, Will's baby things, and her crutches. She watched helplessly as Beatrice loaded the quilt, baby gear, and baby into her car. Then she carefully hobbled out to the waiting vehicle and climbed in, swinging her bad leg in, cautiously.

Will gave an excited crow from the backseat and Meadow was suddenly all smiles. "You get to go to the Patchwork Cottage, Will! You get to see Maisie."

"Kitty!" said Will, grinning and showing off his few baby teeth.

"That's right! What a smart little boy," said Meadow.

Beatrice was just glad that Will was there to cajole Meadow into a better mood. If there was one thing that was unsettling, it was Meadow in a funk.

They walked into the store and headed for the back room where it was set up for the guild meeting with a snack table along the back wall. The room had been where Dan Whitner had started with his painting and it was now a warm yellow. Posy had hung particularly festive quilts on the walls, put some old sewing machines in the corners, and had Dan install a white board. There were two tables set up in an L-shape with folding chairs. It now looked more like a real meeting room.

Everyone oohed and ahhed and Posy gave a pleased smile. "Thanks, everybody," she said shyly.

Miss Sissy had already arrived and immediately took ownership of the baby, plucking him right from Beatrice's arms before anyone else could stake a claim. She'd already lured Maisie the shop cat into the room with cat treats and now she and Will were happily visiting with her.

Meadow found a spot to sit at the table and pushed her chair all the way back so she could keep her leg straight and not have pressure on her ankle. Beatrice handed her the quilt she'd brought and sat down next to her.

"Want me to get you a drink and a plate of food?" asked Beatrice.

Meadow shook her head, looking a bit glum again now that Will was gone. But she quickly switched to a smile when Georgia Potter sat next to her. Georgia, with her pretty features, dancing eyes, and dimples, usually wore tailored clothes but today was sporting a multi-colored, long, flowered dress with meandering seams.

Georgia gave Meadow and Beatrice a smile and looked ruefully at her dress. "It's pretty noticeable, isn't it? But Aunt Tiggy does mean well."

Which was when Savannah walked into the room, wearing a matching dress, although perhaps with slightly better seamwork. She and Georgia exchanged mournful looks before Savannah started speaking with Posy.

Georgia sighed. "Poor Aunt Tiggy. I'm going to host her at my house for the next few days so Savannah can get a break."

It sounded to Beatrice more like "poor Georgia." Beatrice sympathetically asked her, "Too much super-healthy food?"

"Unfortunately. It would be better if it was seasoned, but Aunt Tiggy doesn't seem to use seasoning."

Meadow, who loved a project, suddenly looked engaged again. "You know what Aunt Tiggy needs? Something else to occupy her time."

Beatrice slowly said, "Well, when I saw Tiggy here at the shop, she seemed interested in dating."

Georgia's eyes grew big. "Aunt *Tiggy* did?"

"Yes. Or, at least, she expressed an interest in it."

Georgia said, "Dating *here*? In Dappled Hills?"

"That's right. We asked her the same thing—if she was thinking about settling down here. She said that she would if she was in a relationship," said Beatrice.

Georgia knit her brows. "Wow. Well, that would mean we'd be seeing a lot more of her than we usually do." She quickly added, "I must sound awful. Savannah and I *love* Aunt Tiggy and we're so grateful for how she took us into her home and raised us."

Beatrice smiled at her. "It's just that sometimes there can be too much Aunt Tiggy?"

Georgia gave her a grateful look for understanding. "Exactly."

Meadow was getting more excited. "But, see, if Tiggy is in a relationship, she'll be focused on whoever she's with! She'll transfer all the cooking and sewing to her new husband instead of being focused on you."

Georgia's face brightened. "Do you think so?"

Meadow nodded confidently. "I know so. But now we just need to figure out who would make the perfect match for her. Someone nice."

Beatrice said, "Well, she was interested in Dan Whitner when she saw him here."

Meadow wagged a finger at her. "Doesn't count! He's already in a relationship. I have the feeling Bertha would be none-too-pleased if we were to spirit Dan away from her. I wouldn't want to get on her bad side." She gave a dramatic shudder and looked around her. "She's not here yet, is she? She's our program speaker."

"Not yet," Beatrice said.

Georgia said, beaming, "There should be *plenty* of good, available candidates. This is a great idea, Meadow."

Meadow looked very pleased with herself. "Isn't it?"

Beatrice smiled as Project Tiggy was born. Meadow rubbed her hands together in anticipation of doing some matchmaking. Beatrice knew this would prove an excellent distraction for Meadow and keep her from brooding on her broken ankle.

Posy called the meeting to order and she decided to start out with the sew and tell portion of the program so everyone could share what they were either working on or what they'd finished.

Georgia looked proudly across the room at her sister. "Savannah has something amazing she'd like to share."

Savannah puffed up a little bit. Usually, her quilts were all fairly similar—very well-crafted, but an exercise in precision. She favored neutral colors and geometric patterns for an extremely regimented look.

Meadow muttered under her breath, "Did she do something different this time?"

As Savannah shyly pulled out the quilt, there was a pleased gasp around the room.

"That's amazing," said Beatrice, her gaze running over the finished piece. "How long have you been working on it, Savannah?"

Savannah looked pleased. "Well, it's one of those projects I've been slowly working on for a long time. As you all know,

I've finished several other projects in the meantime, but this is one I worked on once or twice a week."

The quilt was almost an optical illusion of cubes, giving it a feeling of depth and almost of movement. The tops of the cubes were all a neutral cream to give definition, but the exposed sides were in different paisley patterns.

Posy's eyes twinkled. "I was wondering what you were doing with all those paisleys! Savannah this is really marvelous. Are you going to display it at the fair to represent our guild?"

Everyone piped up, urging Savannah to show it. She glanced around the room and then gave a quick bob of her head. "I guess so," she said with a slow smile.

After the room settled down again, they continued with the sew and tell. Beatrice grimaced because she was next. "There's not a great way to follow Savannah's quilt," she said dryly. "And, sadly, I'm *not* working on a quilt that's going to take months and months."

Posy quickly said, "Which is absolutely fine! We don't want everyone to think that we have to have long projects all the time."

Beatrice smiled. "It seems a good deal of my time is being taken up by that little guy, even though it's lots of fun." She gestured across the room at Will, still happily sitting with Miss Sissy and Maisie. The baby gave her a smile in return, showing off his pearly little teeth.

"So here's mine," said Beatrice, standing and displaying a quilt that wasn't a showcase of her talents, but which made her happy. It was a riot of sunny colors in a floral print with a jelly roll jam pattern. "As you can tell, it's an easy pattern and free online. Five-inch squares. I sewed three jelly roll strips together and cut them into blocks."

Everyone gave a pleased murmur. Meadow said, "It puts me in a good mood just looking at it."

They continued through the sew and tell with everyone showing what they'd been working on. Everyone but Miss Sissy, who growled something about quilts being stolen and that there was no use working on new quilts when they might end up disappearing. Or words to that effect.

Posy brought up the fair that coming weekend and talk moved to preparing for that and the display that the Village Quilters was going to have.

Meadow said mournfully, "Of course, I'll be on crutches, which really stinks."

"You're completely absolved from having to do any sort of set-up or take-down of the display area," said Beatrice. "You can just go and enjoy the fair." She was glad again that she'd told Dora Tucker that she wasn't going to help out this time. Every once in a while, it was good to take a break.

The door to the room opened and Bertha stood there, holding a tote bag and hesitating at the door for a minute.

Posy beamed at her. "And here's our wonderful guest speaker today! Hi, Bertha!"

Everyone applauded and Bertha turned a little pink and looked pleased. "Sorry I'm late," she said. "One of my jobs ran a little bit behind."

Posy ushered Bertha up to the front of the room. "Bertha is going to explain to us her method for doing needle turn applique, which she learned from her mom long ago. The flowers she made on these blocks are just beautiful."

Bertha seemed to be warming to the attention and took a quilt out of her bag. The ladies oohed and ahhed and Bertha started explaining how the technique worked.

"Do you make a template?" asked Savannah, always one for getting to the nitty-gritty of how things worked.

Bertha shook her head. "I use a lightbox instead."

Bertha gave a nice little presentation to the group and they applauded again at the end. She grinned at them and made a small bow. "Now, if there aren't any more questions, I've got to run off to another job. Thanks for inviting me!"

She left and Meadow said, "She did a great job. If only she weren't dating Dan! Maybe she'll find greener pastures somewhere else."

Beatrice raised her eyebrows. "You're not thinking of matchmaking *Bertha* now, are you?"

Meadow chuckled. "Who knows? After all, all's fair in love and war."

After the meeting wrapped up, Beatrice headed back home, thinking along the way about the vegetables they had at the house and wondering how best to prepare them for supper. Which is why she was so glad when she walked into the house and saw Wyatt steaming veggies and preparing a fruit bowl.

A couple of quiet days passed by. Beatrice watched Will one of those days and they slipped over to June Bug's bakery to eat some warm doughnuts with sprinkles on them and a chocolate custard filling. Beatrice had started craving them as soon as Wyatt started his diet.

Then, very early Friday morning, there was a phone call from Meadow.

"Is everything all right?" asked Beatrice, still in her robe and slippers. She put her coffee cup down.

"No! Oh, I just can't believe it. How could something like this happen in Dappled Hills? Again!"

Beatrice tried to be patient but that was difficult to achieve when she hadn't yet finished her first cup of coffee. "What happened?"

"Another death!"

Chapter Twelve

Beatrice took a couple of sips from her coffee cup in the hopes of gaining a bit more of the lost patience. "A natural death?"

"No, no, an *unnatural* one. A fisherman called Ramsay a little while ago and I've been stewing ever since. He found a body floating in the lake. And it's Sandra Hughes!"

Beatrice knit her brows. "She drowned?"

"No, apparently her body was dumped there. Ramsay said she was hit on the back of her head with something. That's all he really knows right now, but the state police are looking into it with him. Can you believe it?"

A cold chill went up Beatrice's spine as she realized that she *could* believe it. She'd just had that odd conversation with Sandra a few days ago. But to Meadow, she just mumbled something about it being a terrible shock.

Meadow prattled on another couple of minutes about murderers and wondering how scoundrels could possibly live in a town as perfect as Dappled Hills as Wyatt came over to the table and looked at Beatrice with concern at the early phone call. Beatrice mouthed Meadow's name to him and he nodded.

Then Meadow said, "Well, I should go get dressed and ready for my day. It takes me forever to do anything with this ankle. Talk to you later." And she was gone.

Beatrice filled Wyatt in and he listened to her with a somber expression on his face. "I'm so sorry," he said. "As the pastor of our church, I suppose I might be asked to give a service. But Sandra doesn't have any family here and I'm not positive how to go about reaching them or where they even live. I hope Ramsay can find some information about them."

Beatrice nodded, but her mind was elsewhere.

"Are you all right?" asked Wyatt softly.

Beatrice gave a shiver. "Not really. Sandra knew something. I was speaking with her a few days ago when I took Boris over for his vet visit. She seemed frustrated that the police hadn't made any progress with their investigation into Linton's death. Then she said something about maybe being able to give them a lead."

Wyatt rubbed his face. "Oh, no. So you're thinking that maybe she was killed to prevent the police from finding out who killed Linton?"

Beatrice nodded. "I told her to be sure and tell Ramsay and she said she would. But she must not have been able to before the killer got to her. I should have told Ramsay."

Wyatt gave her a hug. "You didn't know what she knew. And it sounds like she didn't exactly tell you what she knew. There was nothing you could have done—she should have spoken to the police as soon as she could."

"Maybe she wanted to give the killer the chance to explain what she'd seen or heard," said Beatrice slowly. "Or maybe she decided to blackmail them. Although she didn't really seem like the blackmailing type. I just can't picture the vet who was so sweet to Boris pressuring someone like that."

"Or maybe she just got busy with work and put off speaking with Ramsay," said Wyatt softly. "It could just have been as simple as that." He gently changed the subject. "What have you got planned for today?"

Beatrice, still thinking about Sandra, had to stop and remember. "Oh, I've got Bible study this morning. I'll head over to the church with you."

Wyatt fixed them breakfast—eggs and bowls of grits, along with some fruit. Beatrice had more coffee and generally felt more clear-headed afterward. An hour later, they set off.

Wyatt headed into his office at the church after giving her a quick kiss goodbye. Beatrice, who was still a few minutes early, headed to the office to see Edgenora, the church's administrator and fellow guild member.

Beatrice saw Bertha was already in the office and speaking with Edgenora, a rather serious-looking woman in her late-fifties with steel-gray hair and a long, lean build. Bertha quickly asked, "Did you hear the news?"

Beatrice nodded and Bertha looked slightly deflated as if she'd wanted to be the one to tell her about Sandra's death.

"Terrible, isn't it?" asked Edgenora grimly.

"Heard about it at the grocery store before I came by the church," said Bertha. "People sure are talking." She put a hand to her heart. "It's shaken me up—right here."

"But why would someone murder Sandra?" asked Edgenora. "She's always so competent and professional. And a wonderful vet. It's just so unbelievable."

Bertha seemed happy to disabuse Edgenora of the notion that Sandra was completely perfect. "Maybe it had something to do with her relationship with Mr. Hoover. Especially since Mr. Hoover is dead, too."

Edgenora frowned. "Well, that makes sense if just one of them was dead. Maybe one of them had become jealous or became angry after an argument. But with both of them dead?"

Bertha was pleased to offer alternate ideas. "You know, I always got the idea that Brett Hoover was interested in Sandra. And Brett and Mr. Hoover didn't get along, anyway. So maybe Brett was mad about the way Mr. Hoover was treating Sandra . . . they could have gotten into a big fight and it just went a little too far."

Beatrice said, "Was Linton treating Sandra poorly?"

"Course he was! He was running around on her, wasn't he? And they were having arguments and things. Maybe Brett wanted Mr. Hoover to stop being mean to her."

Edgenora said slowly, "But then who killed Sandra?"

Bertha shrugged. "I can't figure all of it out, can I? Maybe somebody else was mad at Sandra and killed her and just hoped the police would blame it on whoever killed Mr. Hoover." Bertha glanced at the clock and said, "Well, guess I'd better get started cleaning up the Sunday school classrooms. Tell Emma I hope she feels better."

Bertha walked out and Edgenora said, "Our Emma has been feeling under the weather so we were able to get Bertha here to clean."

"Hope she's better soon," said Beatrice in a rather distracted voice, still looking in the direction that Bertha had just walked out.

"That Bertha has something of a mouth on her. Not everybody is as bad as she tries to make out, Beatrice. Chin up."

Beatrice turned and smiled at her, appreciating once again Edgenora's sensible nature. "You're right. There's someone in this town that's done something horrible. But there are many more people in Dappled Hills who haven't. Thanks for giving me a better perspective." Switching the subject, she added, "Are you planning on making it to the fair tomorrow?"

Edgenora never seemed much like the festival-going type, but her eyes lit up. "Absolutely. I have a thing for cotton candy and I don't get it nearly enough. My fair plans involve strategic eating at the different food trucks."

"That sounds like fun. I'm hoping to have fun introducing Will to all the fun. I think he'll love it, as long as it's not too loud for him. Sometimes I feel like he has such a quiet life between Meadow and I that he's used to really still environments."

Edgenora quirked a brow. "Meadow? Quiet?"

Beatrice laughed. "All right, maybe that was not quite the correct word to use for describing Meadow."

"I know what you mean, though—he's spending time at houses where there's usually just one or two people there. He's not used to crowds or the sounds of rides. I can imagine it could be overstimulating, for sure."

"Well, we'll see," said Beatrice.

Bertha poked her head back in the office and asked Edgenora, "Sorry, but did you want me also to clean in the gym? I couldn't remember if you said it was used in the last week or not."

"It doesn't really need cleaning, but if you don't mind emptying the trash outside the gym, that would be great."

Bertha ducked back out again and Edgenora called out, "Bertha?"

Bertha looked back in and Edgenora said, "I forgot to ask you . . . do you know anything about Dan's schedule the next week? There are a few small repairs to the property that we'd like to see handled and we thought maybe Dan could take them on."

Bertha rolled her eyes and shrugged. "You know Dan—he can dawdle like the best of them. I'd have thought he was about finished with the Patchwork Cottage by now, but it sure looks like he's got a way to go. You should call him up and ask him."

Edgenora nodded and looked at Bertha carefully. "I'm sorry—I shouldn't have assumed you'd automatically know his schedule. Are you two . . . well . . . are you still seeing each other?"

Bertha shrugged again and gave a sigh. "I don't know. There are a lot of things that I like about Dan. He's a hard worker and he does a good job with everything he does. But he's just so *deliberate*. It takes him forever to get anything done."

"He's a perfectionist?" asked Beatrice.

"That's right. He'll start over from scratch if he sees one thing he just slightly messed up on. He can't finish a project to save his life. I mean, if *I* worked like he did, I'd be cleaning the same house from dawn to dusk. That's no way to earn a living. I try to get him to change what he's doing and stick more to a schedule, but he can't seem to do it." Bertha made a face.

Edgenora said carefully, "That would be very frustrating, for sure."

Bertha bobbed her head. "It's just that kind of stuff that bothers me. He's a great guy, but I'm wondering if he would drive me completely bonkers over time." She dropped her voice as if someone might be somehow listening in. "So I've been thinking we should start seeing other people. But I haven't made up my mind yet."

Beatrice's first thought was that this was excellent news for Savannah and Georgia's Aunt Tiggy. But she did feel badly for Dan to have his relationship taken so lightly. He seemed like a good man.

"I'm off to the gym, then. See y'all later." And Bertha took off again.

A few minutes later, Beatrice left to join up with her Bible study. They'd been working on the book of Jonah, which had more interesting insights than Beatrice had realized. He was certainly someone who had experienced his own share of troubles in life.

Heidi Wheeler was there, looking thin and pale and very subdued. She seemed distracted during the class, looking out the window or down at her hands and not really paying attention to the teacher. Usually, Heidi was the kind of person who enjoyed speaking up, asking questions, and offering opinions. She was always a contributor. But today she sat quietly, looking tired and wan.

After the class was over and people were leaving, Beatrice told the teacher that she'd put the chairs back where they belonged along the wall and Heidi quickly offered to give her a hand. Once everyone had left, Beatrice quietly asked Heidi, "I was just wondering . . . is everything okay?"

Heidi broke down into tears and they both took seats in the two remaining chairs.

Heidi said in a hoarse whisper, "The police keep talking to me. I'm sure they think I killed Linton."

"Why do you think they believe that?" asked Beatrice.

Heidi shrugged. "They think we had some sort of lover's quarrel. Or that I wanted to marry Linton and leave Aiden and that Linton didn't want to marry."

"Is there any truth in that?" asked Beatrice softly.

Heidi looked up at her, tears streaming down her face. "I did want to marry him. I wanted to be with Linton, not Aiden. It's true that Linton didn't want to marry and it's true that we argued over that. I guess someone must have overheard us one day—it was a pretty common argument. I didn't understand why, since we were so happy together, Linton wouldn't want for us to get married."

"Did he offer any reasons why?" Beatrice fished in her purse for a tissue and Heidi gave her a grateful smile.

"Oh, he said the usual kind of thing you'd expect from somebody who had commitment issues. He didn't want to be tied down right then, he was trying to grow his business and wanted to focus on that, or that he didn't want to get married until he could really focus on building a life with someone." Heidi shook her head. "But what it all really boiled down to is that he didn't want to be married. Not to me, not to anybody."

"But you wanted that promise of marriage before you left Aiden," guessed Beatrice.

"Of course. I was going to give up my entire life with Aiden to be with Linton. But I wasn't going to do it unless I was engaged. I had too much to lose, otherwise. And, yes, I was mad at Linton. I started feeling like he was using me. But I never would have *killed* him. I loved Linton." Her voice was subdued and almost flat from exhaustion.

"I suppose you've heard about Sandra," said Beatrice. She gave Heidi a searching look.

Heidi nodded, looking again at the floor. "I did. It's hard to believe. I mean, I didn't like Sandra all that much, but she sure didn't deserve to die. And who does something like that? Kills someone and throws them in the lake? It's just crazy."

"Did you have a good alibi for Sandra's death? I'd imagine that would help keep the police away if you did."

Heidi gave a short laugh. "Well, the police didn't seem any too sure about when Sandra actually died, so I couldn't help them all that much. Even if they *had* narrowed down a time, I was just hanging out at the house, like usual."

"Couldn't Aiden vouch for you?"

Heidi shook her head and looked up at Beatrice. "He was out of town overnight, seeing somebody about a horse we're selling." She furrowed her brow. "Which means that Aiden doesn't have an alibi either. Somehow that didn't occur to me since I've been so worried about myself. Do you think the police will consider him a suspect?"

"Have the police been speaking with him?"

Heidi said helplessly, "I don't really know—like I said, I've barely seen or spoken to him."

Beatrice pressed, "But he does have an alibi for *Linton's* death, right? Even if he doesn't for Sandra's?"

Heidi was quiet for a moment and then slowly shook her head, her eyes meeting Beatrice's. "He wasn't home the morning Linton was found. He wasn't on the farm at all. I just covered for him when the police asked me because I didn't know what else to do."

Beatrice and Heidi sat quietly for a few moments. Then Heidi added, "Beatrice, now I'm wondering if Aiden could have something to do with these deaths."

"What's making you think that?" asked Beatrice. "Aiden seems so calm and stable. Wouldn't something like that be out of character?"

"He is pretty steady, but you know what they say—still waters run deep. I just wonder what he thought about me having an affair with Linton. Linton, especially, I mean." Heidi looked up at Beatrice to see if she understood.

Beatrice nodded. "I hear that the two of them grew up together."

"They were best friends, no matter what Aiden says now. Now he's acting like the two of them were never really close because he's so angry."

Beatrice said slowly, "Heidi, I'm more than happy to talk with you about this. But if there's anything that really makes you suspect Aiden, you should be sure to let Ramsay know."

Heidi pulled back in her chair a little and Beatrice continued in a gentle voice, "He's just trying to figure out what's going on and make sure Dappled Hills is safe for everyone. You can trust him. You've known him your whole life."

Heidi drew in a shaky breath. "Okay. You're right. But right now, there's not really anything I *know*. But I guess I'll let Ramsay know that the alibi I gave Aiden wasn't true. That much I can do."

Beatrice and Heidi finished putting the chairs away and then walked out to the parking lot. Heidi said, "Thanks again, Beatrice, for listening to me. I don't know what I'd do . . . my head just feels like it's spinning all the time. It helps to talk it out."

"I'm so glad," said Beatrice. "And I hope things start looking up for you."

Chapter Thirteen

After church, Beatrice went to the store and picked up one of their deli sandwiches. She still missed her grocery store in Atlanta, but Bub's Grocery had been trying hard lately to create more interesting deli offerings. The sandwich, a BLT, was loaded with a lot more than just bacon, lettuce, and tomato and the bread looked fresh. Beatrice was definitely craving carbs.

When she got back home, she happily ate her sandwich while she took a stab at the crossword in the paper. She'd just finished up the sandwich but not the crossword when her phone rang.

Meadow was on the other end. "Beatrice? Oh, I'm glad I got you. With my ankle and everything, I totally forgot about Ramsay's event!"

Beatrice frowned. "His event? You mean the award he's getting? I thought that was going to be handed out at the fair tomorrow."

"No. I mean, yes, he'll get the writing award at the fair. But this is the writing program he's giving at the library. Remember how I mentioned that?"

Beatrice glanced at the clock. It was right before 1:00. "What time was it supposed to start?"

"Now! Oh, I can't believe it slipped my mind. I was going to try to recruit people to be there. You know how Ramsay is—he didn't say a word to me about it when he left the house today."

Beatrice pushed the crossword away from her. "Are you sure the program is still on—considering he's investigating a case?"

"I'm sure it is. He would have hated to cancel it at the last minute since it's been on the program for so long. It would have let the library down. Besides, it's probably his lunch break. Can you come pick me up and go there with me?"

The prospect of interrupting Ramsay's talk by walking in late wasn't appealing, but neither was the idea of her friend possibly speaking to an empty room. "Of course I will," she said, grabbing her car keys.

A couple of minutes later, Beatrice pulled up into Meadow's driveway. She could see Meadow blocking Boris as he joyfully tried to escape the house and greet Beatrice. Then she hobbled to the car on her crutches and stuffed herself in. "I'll never get used to these things," she grumbled, juggling the crutches and nearly hitting Beatrice in the head with them.

"Just keep them on your side of the car," said Beatrice warily.

The library was a cute building right in downtown Dappled Hills. Beatrice always enjoyed walking in because it had large windows that allowed sunlight in and around the library. The librarians had plants everywhere and were always helpful about finding her something to read. She decided that her next book would *not* be one of Ramsay's picks. She was in desperate need of something a little lighter and easier to read.

Meadow was fussing as they walked to the community room where Ramsay was supposed to be talking. "Poor Ramsay. I just hate that I forgot."

"It might be fine," said Beatrice. "There may be other aspiring writers here. Besides, it would be interesting for readers to listen to the program, too. And Ramsay's a public figure here in town—that alone makes him a draw."

But despite her assurances to Meadow, Beatrice was worried that Ramsay was in an empty room. She was relieved to open the door and see that there were about fifteen people in there—some retirees like Meadow and Beatrice, but also a couple of older teens and various other people.

"Aunt Tiggy is here, too!" whispered Meadow in her loud stage whisper that she fondly imagined to be quiet.

They hurried (or, rather, Beatrice hurried and Meadow carefully persevered) to the back of the room and sat in a couple of chairs in the back row.

Ramsay talked for another twenty minutes, speaking about everything from his own writing process, the importance of support from other writers, writing influences, and how to enter writing competitions.

"And how to *win* writing competitions," Meadow whispered again to Beatrice.

"Shh! It's supposed to be secret," said Beatrice. Although she had to wonder if the news had already gotten out, since the secret was in Meadow's hands.

Then Ramsay opened up the floor to questions. This was another time where Beatrice worried that no one would pipe up, but there were immediately hands that rose. Tiggy's was the first one.

Tiggy stood up and eagerly said, "What is your top tip for establishing a writing habit? I've always wanted to write a book about my grandmother and her life in the country long ago, but I never seem to be able to set aside time to get it done."

"Timers help a lot," said Ramsay. "And setting your goals really low. If you think about the huge project ahead of you—the research, interviews, letters and photos, and the writing—it's too easy to get discouraged and to procrastinate. If you take it one day at a time and break up your project into small, daily tasks, you can really start making progress and keep feeling motivated."

He answered a few more questions about writing. When the questions veered into the territory of his current investigation, he glanced at the clock on the wall of the community room. "Sorry, folks, but I'm going to have to get back to work. Thanks so much to everybody for being here today." He gave a special smile to Meadow and Beatrice as the room applauded. Meadow whistled and cheered and Ramsay turned slightly pink as he hurried back out of the room.

"Wow, he did a fantastic job," said Meadow breathlessly. "I have to say that I'm amazed."

"Well, he knows a lot about writing. He's been doing it for years and has got his process down pat. Plus, he's good at public speaking . . . he's had plenty of practice, after all, with the meetings at town hall."

Tiggy came over and bubbled, "Meadow, you must be so proud of Ramsay. A published author! *And* a police chief at the same time."

Meadow puffed up proudly and said, "Well, I always knew Ramsay had great talent even if I don't always understand what he writes." She gestured to Beatrice. "I think Beatrice does, though."

Beatrice smiled. "I like reading things that challenge me at least some of the time. Of course, Ramsay has me reading Faulkner right now, which is about to burn me out. My next book is definitely going to be a beach read. But Ramsay's short stories are amazing. They always make me look at the world a little differently."

Meadow said wryly, "At least you know what to say after you read them. I always just give him a puzzled look."

Beatrice said, "Tiggy, do you write?"

Tiggy flushed a little and smiled. "Oh, just the little scribbles here and there. But I've always written because it makes me happy. Ramsay has just really inspired me to consider taking my writing a little further."

"Goodness, but you're creative," said Meadow. "Sewing *and* writing?

Tiggy looked pleased. "Did you see the dresses I made for Savannah and Georgia?"

Beatrice and Meadow nodded and carefully didn't look at each other. "We saw them at the guild meeting. The dresses are so sweet," said Meadow.

"I do enjoy sewing, but I think I enjoy writing better. I love sitting down and brainstorming more than figuring out sizes, shopping for fabric, and finding a pattern. And now, living alone and being retired, I have plenty of time to do it."

"Do you *enjoy* being alone?" asked Meadow. She quickly added, "Sometimes I think I'd like a little alone time."

Beatrice thought this was a tactful approach for Meadow. And an unusual one, since Meadow ordinarily plunged into matchmaking whether the person she was matching wanted it or not.

Tiggy gave her a wistful smile. "Well, I'm an independent person, but I've been alone my whole life except when Savannah and Georgia came to live with me and that was long ago. At this point, I'd like to maybe find a companion."

Meadow lit up. "That's what I hoped you might say. I happen to be an excellent matchmaker."

Beatrice looked wearily at her. She'd seen this play out before.

Tiggy, however, looked delighted. "Are you? Oh, Meadow, that would be great. I'm sure you must know everyone in town since you've lived here your whole life. I could use some help." She paused. "I did run into one guy I really liked at the Patchwork Cottage, but he's apparently already spoken for?"

Meadow gave a sniff. "We'll see about that. Who was it?" Apparently, she didn't want Tiggy to think they'd been talking about her.

"He was helping Posy with painting the shop. I think his name was Dan."

Meadow said, "Oh, Dan Whitner. Well, I happen to think you'd be a much better choice of companion for Dan than Bertha."

Beatrice added slowly, "And it's possible that Bertha might be tiring of their relationship. Although I don't know that for sure." However, it had certainly sounded that way when Bertha was talking about Dan in the church office, despite how engaged she seemed with Dan earlier at the Patchwork Cottage.

"Really?" asked Tiggy doubtfully. "She sure seemed like she was attached to him when they were at the shop together."

"Pooh. That was all for show, I bet. Let me see what I can find out."

Beatrice smiled. It was good to see Meadow fired up about a project instead of reflecting on her ankle.

"Thank you! And be sure to tell Ramsay how much I enjoyed his talk today. I'd better head on out—I was going to make a nice healthy lunch for Savannah." And Tiggy hurried out.

Beatrice and Meadow walked out of the library quite a bit more slowly, with Meadow pausing a few times to adjust her crutches. They finally made it down the stairs and to the sidewalk outside. They were about to make their way to the car when some shouting behind them made them stop and turn around.

"What in heaven's name?" asked Meadow, outraged, as they saw Aiden and Brett yelling at each other and then launching into an all-out fist-fight, right there in front of the library and town hall.

There was such a commotion that Ramsay flew out of the police department and launched himself right at the two men with a couple of officers from the state police at his side.

"Whoa!" he shouted. "Stop it, *now.*"

And with that, aside from a little shoving still going on, the two men stopped fighting, panting and glaring at each other.

"The very idea!" said Meadow indignantly. "Fighting in the street. Whatever is Dappled Hills coming to?"

Beatrice and Meadow edged up, wanting to hear what happened but not wanting to get in the way in case the fight started up again.

"What's all this about?" growled Ramsay as the two state policemen held Brett and Aiden apart.

Brett snarled, "You need to be asking Aiden that question. He started bad-mouthing me and then took a swing at me totally out of the blue. Plus, I can tell he's been drinking. That's definitely not helping the situation."

Aiden's face was mottled with anger and he looked sullenly at Brett. But he seemed to be working hard to compose himself.

"Aiden?" asked Ramsay in a stern voice.

Aiden shrugged. "I just had a beer with lunch."

He seemed slightly unsteady on his feet, though, and Ramsay said, "Must have been quite a large beer. What happened with Brett?"

Aiden didn't seem predisposed to answer, so Brett hissed, "He started yelling at me about my 'messed-up family.' I told him I didn't have any control over my brother just like he didn't have any control over his wife."

Beatrice winced. Now it was obvious how the fight had started.

Ramsay winced, too. And the state policeman pulled Aiden a little farther away from Brett since he seemed agitated again. "Okay, that's enough."

Brett brushed himself off. "I'll say. Look, I've got work to do. You know how to find me, Ramsay, if you need me." And he strode away.

Aiden had a small cut on his temple and Ramsay asked, "Either of y'all have a tissue?"

Beatrice pulled one out of her purse and Ramsay handed it to Aiden. "You're bleeding on your temple."

Aiden quietly took the tissue and dabbed at his head. Now that Brett was gone, he seemed like his old self again . . . quiet, unflappable.

The state policemen headed back into town hall.

Ramsay said, "It's not like you to be this way, Aiden. You've always gotten along fine with Brett before. And drinking in the middle of the day like this? What's really going on?"

Aiden was quiet for a few moments, looking down at the ground. Then he said quietly, "You probably know what's really going on, Ramsay. Isn't it your job to know?" He glanced over at Beatrice and flushed. "And I know Heidi has been blabbing to you about everything. Heidi never was able to keep anything a secret."

"You're talking about Heidi's relationship with Linton," said Ramsay.

Aiden snorted. "Relationship. That's what *Heidi* thought it was. I guarantee you that Linton didn't feel the same way. He was using her, I'm sure of it."

Ramsay said, "But Heidi thought they had something more meaningful."

"Of course she did. She's the kind of kid who used to love fairy tales and dressed up as a princess for Halloween." Aiden rubbed his face. He looked completely exhausted. "Look, I know I haven't always been the perfect husband for Heidi. There's a big age difference between us. But there's also the fact that we just don't have a lot of the same interests. I love being outside and staying quiet. She needs more excitement in her life." He shrugged. "I figure that's why she started out on that affair anyway. Just for the excitement of it. Doing something she wasn't supposed to do."

Ramsay nodded. "But then, when you found out about this affair, you weren't exactly happy about it, were you? You always seemed to care about Heidi. I've seen you two together around town over the years. You're always the perfect gentleman with her—opening doors, pulling chairs out for her. You looked like you really doted on her."

Aiden nodded, not meeting his eyes. "That's right."

"How mad were you?" asked Ramsay. "About the affair?"

Aiden looked up at him now, through narrowed eyes. "Not mad enough to kill Linton, if that's what you're talking about. I wasn't happy with the guy, mind you. After all, he and I used to be friends, in a manner of speaking."

Ramsay said, "Well, from what I remember, the two of you were more than just 'sort of' friends. You were very good friends. You were at each other's houses every day, fishing in the lake, going hiking and hunting. I've lived in Dappled Hills for many years, remember?"

Aiden sighed. "Sure, we were good friends. But life changes people. I stayed pretty much the same—the kind of guy who likes to spend time outside, working the land. Linton left Dappled Hills to find better opportunities . . . and I guess he found them. Came back here and then lorded it over all of us. And then he decided he could just act however he wanted to and do whatever he felt like. Including having an affair with someone else's wife."

"But despite the fact that you were really angry with him and you must have felt very betrayed by his behavior, you didn't confront him about it?" Ramsay looked right into Aiden's eyes.

Aiden scoffed. "You don't believe me?"

"Not really, no. That might be due to the fact that you just confronted his brother and he didn't have anything to do with it."

Aiden shrugged and looked uncomfortable. "Might have had something to do with the beer I drank."

"The one beer." Ramsay again gave him a doubtful look.

Beatrice had to agree with Ramsay. Aiden wasn't all that steady on his feet. In fact, he was a bit less steady than Meadow on her crutches. Plus, his face was flushed and not just flushed from fighting.

Aiden sighed. "More than one beer. But it's been a more-than-one-beer kind of week, Ramsay. I'll tell you what I *am* telling the truth about—I didn't have a thing to do with Linton Hoover's death. Nothing. He wasn't worth going to jail over. I'll admit that I was pleased somebody got rid of him, though."

"Any idea who that somebody might be?" Ramsay tilted his head to one side.

Meadow's eyes grew big as if she was about to hear a tremendous secret. She gripped Beatrice's arm.

Aiden shrugged again. "That's not exactly my jurisdiction, is it? More like yours."

"If you had to speculate," pushed Ramsay.

Aiden said, "Well, this is going to sound like sour grapes, but I'd think his brother might have had something to do with it."

"Brett."

"Like I said, I figured it would sound like sour grapes. But Brett and Linton never did get on, even as kids. Those two were about as different as two kids could be. And then you've got the fact that both of them were hotheads. Maybe they had an argument at Linton's house and Linton got rough with Brett, like he sometimes could. Maybe Linton started the fight and Brett ended it."

Beatrice realized that Aiden didn't seem to know exactly how Linton was killed—or he was carefully not admitting to the knowledge. It wasn't like Linton was murdered in the course of a fight. Linton had been hit over the head with a pool cue. It had been a single abrupt blunt trauma to his head.

Ramsay seemed to consider this, too, because he gave Aiden a thoughtful look. "Got it. What do you think they might have been fighting over, if it was Brett?"

"What *didn't* those two fight over?" asked Aiden dryly. "They'd fight over anything, and at the drop of a hat. But what they fought the most over was money."

"Money?" Ramsay perked up at this.

Aiden quickly said, "Realize this has been a long time ago. Like I said, I'd stopped being friends with Linton after he left town. But Brett was always mad that Linton borrowed a lot of money from their dad. Of course there wasn't any contract or anything because their dad treated it like a casual loan. Linton never paid it back and his amount of the inheritance wasn't debited for it."

Ramsay said, "So Brett bore a grudge about this?"

Aiden nodded. "Seemed to. Linton wasn't living here at the time and Brett talked about it a lot the times I saw him. We'd have a drink together once in a while and talk about the old days when we were growing up. But Brett never had anything nice to say about Linton. And now, I should really get going."

"Not in a car, you're not," said Ramsay sternly. "Not with however many beers you've had."

"Heidi is running by to pick me up," said Aiden. "She'll be here in a minute."

"Okay. Well, you take care of yourself. And no more fighting in the middle of Dappled Hills." Ramsay rolled his eyes and walked back into the police station.

Aiden curtly said goodbye to Beatrice and Meadow and left in the opposite direction.

Chapter Fourteen

Meadow looked like she'd just won the lottery. "I think Ramsay forgot we were there! It was a real police interview. And we got all kinds of information! Let's go to June Bug's bakery where we can talk about it. Oh . . . and we could have pastries."

The idea of pastries was suddenly extremely appealing, despite the fact it was past lunchtime. Beatrice was craving carbs again. "Perfect. Let's go."

June Bug's bakery was having a lull, which was nice because it gave Beatrice the chance to catch up with her a little. June Bug, who'd often seemed frantic in the past as she scuttled around from part-time job to part-time job, had really settled in at her bakery. She had Rowesa to help her with the customer-facing part of the job and the cleaning, and that left June Bug able to do the part she loved the best—the baking.

And what an extraordinary baker she was. Beatrice was avidly looking through the glass display case at all the different offerings. Although she'd thought she might want a fruit and cream cheese pastry, she was now leaning toward having a slice or two of cake. After a couple of minutes of not really being able to commit, she finally decided on an apple-cinnamon layer cake with salted caramel icing.

June Bug beamed at her. "That's my new favorite," she said shyly.

"Which one?" asked Meadow. "I don't want to miss out."

So they both ended up with the same cake and June Bug followed them to a table to visit for a few minutes while the shop was quiet. The cake was very rich, so Beatrice decided a single piece was going to have to do. It melted in her mouth and Beatrice closed her eyes briefly. "Mm," she said.

Meadow swallowed down her own piece and said, "This cake is practically criminal, it's so good, June Bug. I clearly need to devote more time to my baking. Once I get my ankle healed up, I'm going to spend my life in the kitchen."

"How's your ankle feeling?" asked June Bug, looking solemn.

Meadow made a face. "It's just not healing up."

Beatrice said, "Meadow, it's only been a couple of days. It's going to take time." And, although she didn't say it, some patience. It was the patience part that was becoming an issue.

"Are you going to be able to make it to the fair?" asked June Bug, her round face crinkling with concern. "You wanted to go; I know."

"I am going to be at that fair no matter what. Beatrice and I want to see Will ride all the baby rides and no one is going to stop me." Meadow's face indicated that it would not be smooth sailing for anyone who tried to stand in her way. Most likely Ramsay.

"As long as you let people know when you're ready to go home and put your feet up," said Beatrice. "Having a set-back isn't going to make you heal any faster, you know."

Meadow, tiring of the subject, immediately jumped to another topic. "June Bug, Beatrice and I wanted to talk about Linton and Sandra."

June Bug's bug-like eyes were sad. "So awful."

"It certainly is. Nothing like this should happen in Dappled Hills. Beatrice has been spending some time looking into it. And Ramsay, of course."

Meadow's voice sounded rather dismissive as she spoke about Ramsay. Beatrice said, "Now, Meadow. Ramsay has been doing a great job trying to get to the bottom of this."

"Yes, but he's so bound up in red tape. That's why you get results faster. Anyway, we were just coming out of the library after Ramsay spoke to a group of aspiring writers. And Brett Hoover and Aiden Wheeler were fighting in the street! Could you hear them from here?"

June Bug's eyes were wide. "No. Should I have been able to?"

"Not if you were baking, maybe. Anyway, they were trying to settle their differences in a very violent manner." Meadow made a tsking sound.

"There were some extenuating circumstances," said Beatrice mildly.

"Because Aiden had been drinking in the middle of the day!"

"I was going to add that stress, for both of them, probably played a part," said Beatrice.

June Bug asked, "What were they mad about?"

Meadow said, "It sounded to me like they insulted each other. That's what caused the fight, anyway. But what Aiden said about Brett was more interesting to me. Didn't you find it interesting, Beatrice?"

Beatrice said, "It sounded like Brett had something of a grudge against his brother."

"It sounded to me that Brett and Linton had *never* gotten along and that the grudge made it worse."

June Bug said slowly, "What was the grudge about? Sad that two brothers couldn't get along."

June Bug, aside from her niece, was all alone in terms of family. Beatrice could understand why she'd find it hard to fathom how someone could push away the family they did have.

"Money," said Meadow distastefully in the same tone she might have used to say *drugs* or *terrorism*.

June Bug's eyes grew even larger.

"Apparently, Linton borrowed money from his father and never paid the amount back. Brett seems to have been upset about it," explained Beatrice.

June Bug gave a solemn nod.

Meadow said in her loud whisper, "So Brett could have argued with Linton over money and then they fought and Brett lost control and killed him!"

"Or, at least, that was a theory that Aiden was floating," said Beatrice dryly. "That's not necessarily what happened."

"It sure does sound like a likely scenario," said Meadow with a sniff. "Then, of course, Sandra saw something and Brett had to kill her, too."

Beatrice thought this over for a moment as she enjoyed a bite of her cake. She finally said, "Sandra really must have seen something—or someone. She told me as much. But it makes sense. After all, she was over at Linton's house early in the morning. She could have seen the killer leaving, or seen some other clue to the killer's identity that we're not aware of."

"But why didn't the murderer kill her right away, too?" asked Meadow. "Wouldn't that have made more sense? After all, for all they knew, Sandra could have gone right to the police. In fact, she *did* go right to the police—straight to Ramsay, the chief. She just obviously didn't tell him exactly what she'd seen."

June Bug suggested in her timid way, "Maybe the killer didn't see her?"

Beatrice said, "That could definitely have been the reason. Sandra might have pulled up just as the killer was leaving and he just didn't notice her because he was in a panic and trying to get out of there. We don't know that the murder was premeditated, so it could be that the killer was shocked by what he did and just wanted to leave the scene as fast as possible."

Meadow nodded. "Sounds about right to me."

"And maybe Sandra didn't say anything to the killer right away," added Beatrice. "So they wouldn't have found out that she'd seen anything until much later."

June Bug looked troubled. "Why wouldn't Sandra go to Ramsay?"

"Well, maybe Sandra was hoping Ramsay would figure it out before she had to tell him. Or maybe she was hoping the person *didn't* do what she thought and she was trying to give them a break. Maybe the person was a friend of hers and she tried to keep it a secret."

Meadow gasped. "Or maybe she wanted to blackmail the person! I mean, vets make plenty of money but maybe Sandra wanted more."

Beatrice said, "The truth is that we really don't know what happened. But it does seem likely that whatever Sandra knew was something that the murderer didn't want anyone else to find out."

The bell on the door rang again and Rowesa started helping the new customer. "I should get back to work," said June Bug. "I'll see you at the fair tomorrow."

"I'll be there!" said Meadow. It sounded like a vow.

The rest of that day and the following morning passed quietly. Wyatt did more healthy cooking which Beatrice, for the most part, enjoyed. Although she still kept having hankerings for sweet or salty carbs.

On Saturday afternoon, Beatrice got a phone call from Meadow. "Want to head over there?" Meadow sounded raring to go.

Beatrice looked at her watch and then at the wall clock to make sure her watch was keeping good time. "Meadow, it's nowhere close to time to go. The fair doesn't even open until six o'clock."

"Ramsay is already there."

"Yes, but Ramsay has to work the fair—traffic, parking, security. He's not there riding the carousel." There was a slight acerbity in Beatrice's tone. She rolled her eyes at Wyatt, who smiled. "Besides, if you go there too early, you're going to get tired out before it even starts. Wyatt and I will give you a call before we come, but it will be right before six." She hung up and rubbed her eyes.

Wyatt said gently, "It's probably the highlight of the week for her."

"Or the highlight of her month. Oh, I get it. She's got major cabin fever at home—she's dying to get out of the house. I'm wondering how long she's going to be able to manage at the fairground, though. What she's talking about doing is a lot . . . going to the award ceremony, hanging out with Will for all the rides, eating."

"She'll probably sleep really well." Wyatt looked thoughtful. "Your mention of eating reminds me that I probably need to eat a big salad before we go so I won't be hungry. It wouldn't be good to be tempted around the food trucks or June Bug's cake table."

"We could take some apple slices with us, too," suggested Beatrice. "Just something small."

Wyatt smiled at her. "You know I've appreciated how supportive you've been with my diet. But this is the local fair and the doctor hasn't told *you* that you need to lose weight. You need to enjoy yourself and have some high-calorie fair food. I'll be fine if I'm not hungry."

She leaned over and gave him a hug. "Thanks. I may have to sneak a funnel cake in. But the last time we went to the fair, I overdid it and a chili cheese dog chased me all night long. So I'm planning on taking it easy, myself. Or at least, avoid greasy food."

Right before six, as promised to Meadow, Wyatt and Beatrice were outside her house and she was eagerly making her way to their car.

Beatrice motioned her to the front seat. "It's easier if I sit in the back. Your crutches will be more manageable in the front."

Wyatt, ever patient and fortunately rather dexterous, still dodged the crutches from the driver's seat as Meadow got in.

Meadow was bubbling with excitement as Wyatt drove to the fairgrounds. "Isn't the weather perfect? Do you remember the other year when the forecasters were disastrously wrong and that thunderstorm raged in? We all had to run to our cars in pelting rain and with lightning striking all around us! I'd never have had a chance if I'd been on crutches then."

"From what I've seen of the forecast, the weather should *stay* perfect. There's not a cloud in the sky," said Wyatt with a smile at Meadow.

Meadow said, "Do you think the baby has already gotten to the fair?"

Beatrice chuckled. "You're making it sound like he drove himself. No, I doubt Piper and Ash are already there. They have all that baby stuff to haul. I've noticed they've had a propensity for running just slightly behind lately."

Meadow looked somewhat deflated and then perked up again. "Well, that will give us a little time to check in with the guild's booth. We *are* supposed to do that."

"Do you have something on display this time, Meadow?" asked Wyatt.

Meadow shook her head. "I felt like I've had a quilt or two on display for so many years that it was time for some new voices."

"New voices? From our group?" asked Beatrice doubtfully. Their guild members had all been quilting for many years.

"Okay, maybe not *new* voices. But voices that don't pipe up enough. I was excited about Savannah's quilt. It was very radical for Savannah, you know."

Beatrice said, "I totally agree. It still was in keeping with her overall theme of order and symmetry, but had so much depth and movement to it."

Meadow turned in her seat to grin at her. "I love it when you start sounding like an art museum curator."

"I do, too," said Wyatt, his eyes twinkling in the rear-view mirror at her.

Minutes later, Wyatt pulled up to the entrance of the fairground, right by the admissions gate. "I'll let you two off here so Meadow won't have to walk from the far end of the parking lot."

"We'll probably be at the Village Quilters' booth, but text me if you don't see me," said Beatrice, climbing out of the car.

Meadow also clambered out and wobbled on her one foot as she struggled to get the crutches out and under her arms. "Okay, ready!" she said finally, eyes gleaming.

Wyatt drove the car away and they bought their admission. Meadow said, "I'd like to buy some tickets for the rides."

The fair attendant gave her a doubtful look. "You sure about that? Some of those rides are pretty fierce." He gestured behind him to an illuminated ride where the capsules the riders were in swung all the way around on what looked like mechanical spider arms. They could hear the happy screaming from it. Actually, spinning appeared to be a favorite element in the rides. There were rides that spun close to the ground and rides that spun in the air. It made Beatrice feel slightly sick just looking at them. "Maybe the bumper cars would be all right, if you wanted to try those."

"Oh, no. I'm going to ride the baby rides with my grandbaby," said Meadow placidly.

"You won't need a ticket for those," said the attendant. "And you won't be able to go on all of them. Some are just for the little guys."

After much discussion, they didn't buy any ride tickets. "It's a good thing he stopped you," said Beatrice. "I can't imagine how many tickets you'd have bought otherwise."

"I'd have bought them by the yard," said Meadow cheerfully. "Now you're going to help me keep track of time, right? We can't miss Ramsay getting his award. And he's going to do a reading, too."

Beatrice raised her eyebrows. "A reading? I didn't realize that."

"Yes, and I can tell you he was *so* nervous when he left home. He must have practiced a dozen times."

Beatrice said, "But he's so good at public speaking. He just spoke yesterday at the library and looked totally at ease."

"That's true, but he didn't share any of his work. He just spoke about *writing*. Sharing something he's written in public is very different, apparently. He said it's like allowing people to look into his head." Meadow shrugged. "I don't totally get it, but I know he's anxious about it."

They walked over to the Village Quilters' booth and saw Savannah there, proudly standing in front of her quilt. "I hope you get a prize," said Beatrice. "You certainly deserve one."

Savannah flushed and gave Beatrice a big grin. "Do you really think so? That means a lot, coming from you."

"It's the best thing I've seen you do and it's different from anything else here. It's going to really stand out to the judges," said Beatrice confidently.

"You'll need to make sure you're at the main stage when the judges announce the winners," said Meadow excitedly. "And it wouldn't be a bad idea to be there earlier for the other prizes, you know. Just in case someone else gets an award of some kind."

Savannah said, "Are *you* getting one, Meadow?"

"No, and I'm not allowed to say who is. But try to be there!" Meadow gave a quick glance around her and said, "How are things going with Tiggy?"

Savannah grinned. "Much better now that she's staying at Georgia's house for a while. I've been eating all the junk food I can inhale since she's been gone. Catching up for lost time, you know."

Beatrice pointed at Savannah's outfit. Although hardly fashionable, it was definitely the sort of tailored garment that Savannah usually wore. "It looks like you're back to wearing your own clothes, too. At least, that doesn't seem to be a Tiggy name brand."

"Oh, I wore the dress she made yesterday and that's my excuse for not wearing it tonight at the fair, since it's in the hamper. I can't bear to hurt her feelings but that dress was not exactly a fair-going garment," said Savannah ruefully.

"Well, this will make you smile. I have an idea for the perfect match for Tiggy!" said Meadow.

"Who is it?" asked Beatrice and Savannah at the same time.

"Mr. Tillsdale!" Meadow beamed at them as if waiting for the accolades.

"Mr. Tillsdale?" asked Beatrice slowly. "Isn't he a good fifteen or more years older than Tiggy?"

"He's reliable. And routine-driven, just like Tiggy."

Savannah asked, "Does he ever say anything? I'm not sure I've ever heard him speak."

"That's what makes him especially perfect. Tiggy likes doing things her way and Mr. Tillsdale wouldn't dream of contradicting her."

Beatrice shook her head. "I don't know, Meadow. I just don't see it. I think you might need to go back to the old drawing board."

Meadow heaved a melodramatic sigh. "But that's the problem—there aren't that many eligible bachelors in Dappled Hills right now. At least not of a particular age or someone I'd feel all right about Tiggy getting involved with. There's Roger Wilson, I suppose."

Meadow didn't sound at all enthusiastic about Roger Wilson. Beatrice frowned. "I don't think I know him."

Savannah said, "Isn't he the one who doesn't really leave his house?"

"I'm sensing a theme with this," said Beatrice. "Quiet people."

Meadow said, "Well, if Dan Whitner would just cooperate then I wouldn't have to even consider dragging all the recluses out from their homes and forcing them to date Tiggy!"

Savannah said slowly, "Dan Whitner? Isn't he the guy who's been at the Patchwork Cottage doing all the handywork and painting and all?"

Meadow nodded.

"Wasn't he dating Bertha?" asked Savannah. "I saw them out together at lunch a couple of times."

Beatrice said, "They've been dating for a while, apparently."

Savannah gestured across the fairground. "Well, maybe they're not really dating anymore."

Meadow and Beatrice followed her gesture across to where Bertha was hanging on the arm of a man who definitely wasn't Dan Whitner. They appeared to be sharing cotton candy and she was laughing into his face. The man gave her a kiss and she happily returned it. Beatrice remembered that Dan's days had sounded numbered when she'd spoken with Bertha in the church office, but this seemed like very fast work indeed.

Meadow looked ecstatic. "Oh! That's *wonderful*. Oh, Savannah, thanks for being so very observant. It's much better for Tiggy to be with the man she wanted to be with all along. This couldn't be more perfect. Now we just need to let Tiggy know. She'll be so delighted."

"Just remember that Dan might want to take things slow," said Beatrice. "And Tiggy might, too. I'm guessing she hasn't been in a relationship for a while."

Savannah said sadly, "I don't think she's really *ever* been in a relationship. Her whole life was her job and now that she has stopped teaching, she needs something else to focus on. I was getting worried that Georgia and I were going to be her focus."

"Maybe she needs a coach," said Meadow, again getting that gleam in her eye that meant she had a project underway.

"Now, Meadow," said Beatrice. "There's something to be said for keeping out of people's business."

Meadow bobbed her head. "You're so right, Beatrice, as always! He *might* be on the rebound and this might be super-easy, even for Tiggy."

Beatrice sighed as Meadow missed the point once more. She wondered how Meadow could still have so much energy when Beatrice was starting to feel very tired, herself.

Fortunately, Wyatt joined them then. "Ready to meet up with Piper, Ash, and Will? I just spotted them coming in after I parked the car."

Meadow clapped her hands, all thoughts of matchmaking or relationship coaching completely gone. "Yes! I've been looking forward to this for weeks."

Chapter Fifteen

Piper and Ash had thoughtfully waited to go on the rides until the grandparents could join them. Instead, they were showing Will award-winning drawings from the local elementary school in a booth where the very best were on display. The young artists were in the booth too, proudly showing off their drawings and paintings. Will looked like he was drinking it all in, his gaze going from one brightly colored piece of artwork to another while his parents chatted with the kids.

"You'll have to start him finger painting," said Meadow, her thoughts already clearly going in a familiar direction—that Will was a prodigy and just needed the right tools to create a masterpiece.

Piper and Ash gave them hugs and Will grinned his fetching partially-toothed grin at them.

"Ready to do some rides?" Piper asked Will.

Will looked uncertainly at the big, scary, spinning rides that the man at the admissions booth had warned Meadow over.

"No, they have special rides for boys and girls your age," said Piper, reading his mind. "And we'll be right there."

Beatrice said, "Maybe we should start off with the carousel." She couldn't think of a gentler ride to start Will off on and it was one where an adult could get on too and hold onto him. "That should ease his mind a little bit."

They decided that was the best starting place and headed over. Will was turning his head from side to side as Ash carried him, looking at the different people, listening to the different sounds, and smelling the unfamiliar foods. There were bright lights and lots of laughing. Beatrice thought it could so easily be overwhelming, but Will seemed to be taking it in stride.

When they reached the carousel, Will showed no reluctance about getting on the ride, making a delighted crowing sound as soon as he spotted it.

"Want to pick out a horse, love?" asked Beatrice and Will ran all the way around the ride, looking up at the majestic painted horses. He finally settled on a black one that seemed to be smiling slightly as if it were in on a joke that no one else understood.

Beatrice rode with him . . . or rather, stood next to him and held him on the steed (who, according to its saddle, was named Titan). Meadow wanted to go, but it was decided that crutches and general unsteadiness would not be a good match for a carousel. Meadow, Wyatt, and Ash were the cheerleaders who called out, "Yay, Will!" every time he circled around and Piper took pictures. Will and Beatrice waved graciously each time they swung around to face them.

Will was so enamored with the ride that he chortled out, "More!" whenever it stopped. So began Will's long ride on the carousel.

"I'll get more tickets," said Ash with a wry air of resignation.

Ash rode with Will on the next ride and then Piper took a turn. Wyatt, Beatrice, and Meadow were standing and waving when they heard a voice behind them.

They turned to see Brett Hoover standing there with a very official-looking camera.

"Taking some photos for the event?" asked Wyatt.

Brett nodded and Meadow's eyes immediately lit up.

"Will you take some of our grandson? It would be wonderful to have an *official* photo of Will."

He smiled at her. "That's what I was going to ask . . . if I had your permission to snap a few pictures."

"You absolutely do," said Meadow fervently.

And so Brett started clicking off photos with Piper and Will waving and smiling at him.

"Where will the picture run?" asked Beatrice.

Brett said, "I'm doing some freelance work for the paper, so it will definitely run in there. And it might also be on promo materials for next year's fair." He looked as if he was trying to sort out what to say next. "I'm glad I ran into y'all tonight—I was hoping I would. I wanted to apologize to y'all for my behavior the other day." He glanced at Wyatt. "You probably heard about it from Beatrice."

"She mentioned something about it," said Wyatt mildly.

Brett took a deep breath. "Obviously, I'm not happy about it. I don't usually start fighting with people right in the middle of downtown. Anyway, I'm sorry you had to see that."

"It's no problem at all," said Beatrice.

Brett shook his head. "Well, it's been weighing on me. I haven't been acting like myself lately and I think it's mostly due to stress."

Wyatt looked concerned. "I hope it's not work stress. We can extend the amount of time for the pictorial directory photos, if you need more time."

"Oh no, I'm actually finishing those up tomorrow. No, it's been more personal stress than anything else. I was upset to hear about Sandra."

Wyatt nodded and said, "I'm sure you spent some time with her since she was dating Linton."

Brett said, "I did. She'd phone me sometimes and talk about Linton; he wasn't treating her right. She'd share problems with me just like I was a brother of hers. And she was often frustrated by Linton, of course. Just like I was." He took a deep breath. "Sandra tried to phone me that night she died. But I couldn't pick up because I was at a gig."

"A gig?" Meadow's brow furrowed.

"I was taking pictures at a rehearsal dinner. I've been working a lot lately, piecing together work at a lot of different venues. Anyway, I saw the call come in, but couldn't answer it because I was working. The rehearsal dinner ran long and late and by the time I got off work, it was too late to call her."

Beatrice asked, "What did you think she was calling about?"

Brett shrugged and looked serious. "Well, I figured it was just a normal conversation—that she wanted to reach out to talk about Linton and how she missed him. That sort of thing. Before Linton died, she'd call and talk about how Linton was cheating on her or how Linton brushed her off or ignored her texts or phone calls. After he died, she'd talk more about how she felt alone now that he was gone. I thought I could call Sandra back the next morning and we'd just talk then."

"Did she leave a message?" asked Wyatt.

Brett shook his head. "No. And then, of course, I heard that she'd been found in the lake. I couldn't believe it. Now I have to wonder if she was calling me because she was in trouble of some kind. From what I understand, she was murdered, right?"

Meadow nodded immediately, never one to keep information close to her chest.

Brett sighed. "I can't help but feel guilty. Maybe I could have helped her somehow. Maybe her call was an SOS."

Wyatt said, "There's probably nothing you could have done. Try not to blame yourself. Instead, feel good that you were a friend who helped her out and provided an ear when she needed it."

Brett looked unconvinced but nodded.

Beatrice said, "Did Sandra talk about Linton's death at all in terms of the murder itself? Did she have any ideas about who might have killed him? Did she know anything?"

Brett gave her a sharp look. "You think she knew something and the killer murdered her before she could talk?"

Beatrice said, "It made me wonder."

Brett considered this for a moment and then said slowly, "Not really. Or maybe I wasn't really paying attention. I mean, I was totally focused on her and listening when she was talking usually, but sometimes she said kind of esoteric things and I'd zone out for a minute."

"Esoteric?" asked Meadow.

"Maybe just 'random' would be a better word. She'd kind of ramble. I used to think it was a self-comforting mechanism or something. Anyway, the only thing I can think of that she mentioned in relation to his murder was something about a quilt."

"A quilt?" asked Beatrice and Meadow in chorus. They gave each other an uneasy look.

"Yes," said Brett, his eyebrows furrowed. "Does that mean anything to you?"

"It seems like an odd thing in relation to Linton, that's all," said Beatrice quickly. If Miss Sissy's quilt had anything to do with Linton's death, she didn't feel like she should mention it now.

Brett nodded absently. "Sure didn't fit in with the rest of his décor, that's for sure."

"What do you think?" asked Beatrice. "Do you have any thoughts on what might have happened to either your brother or Sandra?"

Brett's expression darkened. "No. If I did, I'd be confronting somebody about it. Or going to the cops. But I do know somebody who's getting on my nerves from a variety of different angles and that's Heidi Wheeler."

"What happened with her?" breathed Meadow.

"Nothing, really. But she came to the church to get her photo snapped for the pictorial directory. Aiden wasn't with her—she'd said he couldn't make it because he had something important that he had to do on the farm." He looked at Wyatt. "You know how the photo sessions usually are."

Wyatt cleared his throat. "Yes. They're pretty cut-and-dried, aren't they? Folks come in, they sit, you tell them how to pose, and you snap a couple of pictures."

"That's right. But Heidi seemed to want to talk. In fact, she seemed *desperate* to talk. It was almost like she didn't have an outlet anymore, or anyone to talk with." He shrugged.

Beatrice thought about how Heidi had seemed the same way with her. She'd definitely wanted someone to listen to her. But then, it had sounded as if Aiden was barely speaking to her at home, especially since he'd found out about her affair.

"Was it just chit-chat then?" asked Meadow. "Or something more?"

"She wanted to talk to me about Linton. Honestly, it was almost like Sandra talking to me about Linton—how much she missed him and how alone she felt. But it was something that I didn't want to hear from her. She was also really throwing shade at Sandra," said Brett.

"Throwing shade?" asked Beatrice.

"Sorry. I meant that she was saying unpleasant things about her. Acting like everything was Sandra's fault . . . that Sandra had been trying to force Linton into a relationship that he didn't want, blah, blah, blah. I was just trying to do my work and get her photo taken." Brett rolled his eyes.

"That must have been frustrating," said Beatrice.

"Oh, it was. Plus, I was really trying to bite my tongue to keep from telling her off. I just didn't think it was the time or the place to go off on her. Then she started talking about how she and Linton had all these plans for the future and something just snapped in me. I told her that if she had really wanted Linton for herself, she should have divorced Aiden and then convinced Linton to marry her. I said that Sandra had nothing to do with keeping them apart. And I said that Linton, as far as I was aware, had absolutely no intention of getting married. He liked the single life too much."

"I'm guessing Heidi didn't enjoy hearing that," said Beatrice dryly.

"No. In fact, she stormed right out and I had to pick out one of the pictures I'd already taken for the directory. And it wasn't very flattering." A slight smile tugged at Brett's mouth.

Meadow was pink with indignation. "Well, she completely ambushed you. Talking to you about your brother and her personal life while you were working. And at church!"

Brett shrugged again. "Like I said, she seemed really desperate to talk." He chuckled. "And y'all must think I'm desperate to talk, too, because here I've been, talking your ears off. I really just wanted to take a picture of your grandson and apologize for the other day. Thanks for the picture—it's going to look great in the paper."

Meadow watched Brett as he left. "That young man has a lot on his shoulders right now." She frowned. "Isn't he supposed to have a funeral or a memorial or something soon?"

Beatrice shook his head. "That's not what he wants, at least right now. He called Wyatt at the church to tell him so."

Meadow said, "They really *didn't* have a good relationship, then."

Piper and Will joined them and Piper said, "Well, I think we're finally done with the carousel."

"At least it will be memorialized forever in the newspaper," said Wyatt with a smile.

"I think I'd be a little dizzy if I'd gone around and around that many times," said Beatrice.

Piper chuckled. "I still feel like I'm on it."

Ash joined them. "I think I'm good with tickets now." He showed them the tremendous mound of tickets that he'd purchased.

"Considering how obsessed Will got with the carousel, I think it's good to be overprepared," said Piper. "What other rides do they have?"

"Oh, let's try the little airplanes next," said Meadow. "If he likes going around and around, that will be perfect for him!"

Will did love the airplane ride. In fact, he now appeared completely fearless and waved confidently at them from his perch in the bright blue airplane that circled slowly around several feet off the ground.

"He looks like a miniature pilot," said Beatrice with a laugh as they all took pictures.

A couple from church approached Wyatt and spoke to him for a while as Will proceeded to ride the plane for several more rides.

Piper said, "Would y'all mind watching Will for us so that Ash and I can grab something to eat?"

Meadow grinned. "We thought you'd never ask! Yes, we want Will all to ourselves, don't we, Beatrice?"

Ash gave Meadow a worried look. "How's your ankle, doing, though? You're not overdoing it, are you?"

"Not a bit! It's never felt better," said Meadow stoutly.

Beatrice, however, noticed that Meadow seemed to be walking a bit more stiffly than she had been as they moved on to the next ride they wanted Will to try—a little train that was another solo small child ride. Armed with the large roll of tickets Ash had given them, they approached the train.

"Which car do you want to sit in?" asked Beatrice.

"Boo one," said Will automatically, heading for the blue car and climbing in.

As the train slowly started off, Beatrice said, "Oh, Miss Sissy's coming over."

Meadow murmured, "Really?" in an absent voice as she continued snapping photos of her grandchild.

Miss Sissy came right over, holding a large amount of food and scanning the ride with narrowed eyes. Her face lit up and her eyes danced when she finally spotted Will. She waved enthusiastically at him with an arthritic hand and the little boy gleefully waved back. When the train ride was over, he got off and trotted over to them. "More!"

"Another ride?" asked Beatrice.

Miss Sissy leaned down. "Here," she said gruffly to Will.

He happily took the chocolate bar she handed him.

Beatrice counted off several tickets and said, "Will, hand these to the ticket lady."

Will carefully reached up and handed her the tickets before getting back into the blue car. As the train started off, he grinned conspiratorially at Miss Sissy and started eating his chocolate.

Meadow said, "Are you enjoying the fair, Miss Sissy?"

The old woman hissed at her, "Bad man."

Meadow gasped and looked around fiercely as if the afore-mentioned bad man better have the good sense to stay out of her way. "Where? Where is he?"

"*Ramsay* bad man," stressed Miss Sissy, glaring at her.

"What on earth did he do this time?" asked Meadow as if Ramsay was continuously doing inappropriate things.

"Asking questions," muttered Miss Sissy, scowling. Her features brightened as Will circled around and she waved at him again.

Beatrice said, "Asking questions about the murders? That's part of his job, though."

Miss Sissy snorted.

Meadow said, "Beatrice, I'm with Miss Sissy on this one. Ramsay should certainly know better. It's Miss Sissy! What danger could she be to anyone?"

Beatrice wasn't sure, but she knew she never wanted to be on the old woman's bad side.

Meadow looked at her watch. "After Will rides a couple more times, we're going to need to be heading over to the award tent." She smiled at Miss Sissy. "Do you want to come with us? We might see people we know getting awards."

The expression on Miss Sissy's face indicated that watching people get awards was considerably less-interesting than eating fair food or waving at Will on the train ride. "Will the baby be there?"

"No, well, probably not. He likely wouldn't find it very interesting. We'll probably drop him off with Piper and Ash for a little while."

"Hmph," said Miss Sissy as a response. It seemed like a no to Beatrice.

Chapter Sixteen

And, in fact, Miss Sissy trotted off with Piper and Ash as soon as they came back and Will was finished with the train ride. Wyatt broke away from his conversation with the church member and joined Beatrice. Ash said to Meadow, "Take plenty of pictures of Dad getting the award, please. I'm going to pop in the back for a few minutes to try to see it, but I won't be close enough for pictures. Just trying to make sure Piper doesn't have to wrangle Will by herself at the fair for too long."

"I'll take gobs of them," said Meadow, beaming. "It isn't every day that a member of our family wins an award. But I bet that will change when Will gets a little older!"

Ash gave Beatrice a wry look and then said to his mother, "We'll see, Mama. He's just a baby, you know."

"A very bright baby!" said Meadow as Piper, Ash, and Will headed off.

There was a central tent with a stage where most of the entertainment was being held. There they had folk musicians, bluegrass bands, square dancers, and the awards for best produce and livestock as well as awards in the arts and crafts.

Beatrice, Wyatt, and Meadow entered while a local folk duo was singing and clapped enthusiastically after they were done.

"They are so talented," said Beatrice, shaking her head. "I wish I could sing."

"Can't you?" asked Meadow in surprise. "You do almost *everything* well."

"Not sing," said Beatrice ruefully. "You wouldn't want to hear me attempt that. And you know my cooking is far from extraordinary."

Meadow tilted her head to one side. "No, it's always good."

Wyatt smiled at Beatrice. "I agree. I always enjoy it."

"It's very pedestrian, but it's nice for you two to say that."

"Maybe it's because you're always so organized and efficient. It makes you seem like you can tackle anything," said Meadow thoughtfully. "Oh, look! I think this is Ramsay's award."

But it wasn't, yet. The rather nerdy, academic-looking group that had taken the stage were awarding the prize to the elementary-aged children who'd entered the art contest. The kids excitedly took their ribbons when their names were called.

Then an elderly lady with a commanding appearance took the stage.

"I think this is going to be for the quilts," said Meadow. "I recognize her from past years. I hope Savannah wins something."

Beatrice peered around. "Where *is* Savannah? I didn't see her or I'd have sat with her. And where's Ramsay?"

Meadow frowned, her gaze scanning the crowd by the stage. "I don't see either one of them. For heaven's sake, you'd think they'd be able to take a break from whatever they're doing to get an award. And Ramsay's supposed to be giving a reading!"

The elderly woman did indeed introduce herself as the judge for the quilt show portion of the fair. She listed off the winners and there were cheers as each was announced. Savannah was one of the winners and Beatrice, Wyatt, and Meadow cheered loudly.

"Look, there she is," said Beatrice. "We just couldn't see here because that big man was blocking her."

Savannah, blushing radiantly, took her award and looked shyly around the tent as they continued to cheer. After she got her ribbon, she joined them.

"Congratulations!" said Meadow, giving Savannah a big hug as she joined them.

"May I see your ribbon?" asked Beatrice. Savannah proudly showed her a large blue ribbon, the first she'd ever won.

"It's beautiful," said Beatrice and Savannah flushed happily again.

"Is Ramsay about to get his award?" asked Savannah. "I didn't want to miss it."

Meadow craned her head to look around the crowded tent again. "It's got to be coming up. They gave him an estimated time for him to be receiving the award since they knew he was going to be working, but it's already past that. I just can't believe he's not here!"

Beatrice said in a soothing tone, "He might be here. We couldn't see Savannah, either, behind that large man."

"Yes, but Ramsay *is* a large man. I don't think anybody would be obscuring him here." Meadow was starting to look fretful.

Another academic-looking group of people took the stage and Meadow whispered, "This is it, for sure! The judges for the writing contest. How awful. Should I accept his award for him? But I can't read his work for him! Oh, goodness."

Beatrice turned to look all the way in the back and said, "Look, Meadow—he's standing at the door now. He must have gotten interrupted by something at the fair."

It was perfect timing. The judges announced his win and he strode to the stage in full police regalia with everyone clapping and Meadow whistling and taking pictures.

He did look a bit nervous, especially for someone who'd easily given such a natural and informative talk at the library just the day before.

One of the judges said, "And now Ramsay Downey will be reading his winning flash selection for our enjoyment."

The judge backed away from the microphone and Ramsay stood in front of it. He cleared his throat and smiled at the audience and Meadow let out a cheer. Then he took a deep breath and started reading the short piece that had won him a ribbon. It was in the mystery category and was a twisty tale with an unreliable narrator. Beatrice glanced around at the audience, worried that they might be distracted during a reading, but most of them seemed intent on his words as he read through the work. When he finished and gave the surprise ending, there was a lot of applause.

Ramsay looked surprised and gratified and bobbed his head in acknowledgement before quickly heading off the stage and toward the exit.

"Let's join him," said Meadow to Beatrice and Wyatt.

"Tell him congratulations for me," said Savannah. "I'm going to stick around here to watch the next musical group."

When they got outside, Meadow gave Ramsay such a ferocious hug that she dropped her crutches altogether. Beatrice picked them up for her and handed them back to her. Ash had gotten there in time to see Ramsay get the award and he gave him a hug, too, congratulating him before rejoining Piper and Will.

"Did I do all right?" asked Ramsay, looking a little anxious.

"You were marvelous!" said Meadow.

Wyatt said, "I agree with Meadow. I looked around the audience while you were reading and they looked riveted. You did a wonderful job."

Ramsay gave a relieved sigh. "I'm glad. I spent enough time practicing that short story. I think I could recite it from heart."

He showed them his award, which was a small, engraved plaque.

"We'll put it in a place of honor," said Meadow stoutly. "Where everyone can see it."

Ramsay said, "I was thinking we'd hang it somewhere in our bedroom, Meadow. We don't really need to have it on public display."

Meadow put a hand on her hip, again making a crutch fall to the ground. "It's not every day that a member of this family gets an award. I think it deserves to be recognized." She frowned. "By the way, I wanted to ask you something. What on earth did you do to Miss Sissy today?"

Ramsay gave her a wary look. "Miss Sissy? Nothing."

"Then why did she call you a bad man?" demanded Meadow.

Ramsay snorted. "Because she's a difficult woman who doesn't like answering questions—even necessary questions. You know I handled her with kid gloves, but I had to speak with her about Sandra Hughes."

"What on earth could Miss Sissy have to do with Sandra's death? I can *sort* of see you questioning her about Linton because she had that altercation with him. But Sandra?" Meadow's expression indicated that she thought Ramsay had completely lost his mind.

"Now, Meadow," said Ramsay. "It was completely necessary. Miss Sissy was spotted by someone having an argument with Sandra."

"Miss Sissy argues with *everyone*!" Meadow's eyes flashed.

Beatrice bit her lip to keep from smiling. Meadow was right, but it still didn't look good.

"Yes, but she doesn't call everyone a thief. It was more of a confrontation than a mere argument. Miss Sissy was apparently rather upset."

Beatrice said, "What was it that Miss Sissy was accusing Sandra of having stolen?"

Ramsay sighed. "The quilt, of course. I think the station's done with it and we need to get it back to her. I told her that we had it, but I suppose Miss Sissy forgot and then thought Linton and Sandra were in cahoots together to take the quilt." He looked at Beatrice. "And you were right, of course—it's a pretty valuable quilt."

He glanced at his watch. "I'd better get back to patrolling the fair. Beatrice, do you mind putting the plaque in your purse?"

"I can take it," said Meadow. "I'll take good care of it."

"If you put it in your purse, Meadow, you'll be even more unstable on those crutches than you already are. Are you sure you don't want to head back home now? You've had some fair food, you've watched Will on the rides, and you've seen me get my award. There's nothing much else to do, surely." He handed the plaque over to Beatrice and she put it carefully in her purse.

Meadow made a face. "There's plenty to do, silly. I bet Will is going to ride the rides all over again . . . you should have seen how much fun he was having. But thanks for looking after me, sweetie." She gave him a peck on the cheek and they waved as he headed off into the rides area.

"Let's go catch up with Piper and Ash," said Meadow.

And that's what they did. Will did indeed want to repeat his magical experience on the baby rides. He didn't seem as though he'd ever wear out or tire of them. But he discovered that his *parents* could wear out and tire of them.

Piper said, "Ash, we'd better go ahead and head out. It's late and he's going to be totally wiped out soon. I think he's running on fumes now."

Ash looked at his watch. "I'll say. Besides, it's always better to leave when he's still happy instead of after the meltdown hits."

"Pooh," said Meadow. "Y'all are party poopers."

"We sure are," said Piper with a chuckle. "I don't mind saying that as soon as I tuck Will in, I'm heading to bed myself. I'm totally exhausted. I'll leave the fair to you young people."

Ash said, "Although you should be turning in, too, Mama. You really need to rest that ankle. It's looking a little swollen to me."

Meadow quickly rejected this idea. "Nonsense! It's my pants—they're making my leg look bigger."

Beatrice rolled her eyes at Ash, who chuckled.

"All right, Mama. But promise me you're not going to push it too much. Who's taking you home tonight?"

"I think I want to stay until the bitter end with Ramsay. I haven't seen much of him what with this case and with him working the fair and then getting the award. I'd like to ride back with him."

Ash frowned. "But he's going to be shutting *down* the fair. Directing traffic out and all that. That's way too long for you to be standing."

Wyatt said quickly, "I'm happy to shuttle you back home, if you'd like."

Meadow sniffed. "I know of a perfectly good set of benches that are close to the parking lot. I'll be just fine there until Ramsay's done. I can watch the fair workers pack up the rides. It'll be most entertaining."

There was really no changing Meadow's mind once it was set. Ash recognized the futility of trying and he and Piper set off for the car with Will in tow. A couple from the church walked up to Wyatt and engaged him in conversation.

Beatrice said, "So what now? I don't see myself staying much longer now that our primary reason for being here has just toddled off. Maybe just until after Wyatt finishes speaking with those folks. There's not a whole lot here that we haven't covered."

Meadow considered this and then smiled. It was a smile that Beatrice had come to distrust.

"I know. We can try to get Tiggy and Dan connected. We just have to figure out where they both are."

Beatrice said, "I'll leave the matchmaking to you, Meadow. But as far as where Tiggy is, my guess would be that she's either at the Village Quilters' booth or hanging out with Posy at her vendor booth. It's what makes the most sense, since she really doesn't know anyone here."

Meadow narrowed her eyes. "And I think I've just spotted Dan. He's looking rather forlorn, isn't he? So we can help *everybody* out."

"Are you sure that catching Dan on the rebound is a good idea?"

Meadow said, "He seems like the kind of guy who likes being in a relationship. And, if he can't be in the one he's just been dumped from, he might as well explore another one. Besides, Tiggy really liked him, right?"

Beatrice had to agree that had appeared to be the case.

"Then let's go!" Meadow thumped off toward Dan, crutches working furiously as she set off, a woman on a mission. Wyatt, still talking to the couple, smiled as Beatrice gave him a rueful look as she followed Meadow.

"Dan! Yoo-hoo!"

Dan turned around, looking startled. "Me?"

Meadow laughed. "Of course, you. Goodness, how many Dans do we know? Not very many! It looks like you're wandering around on your own tonight."

"Yes, well, that's just the way things have worked out," said Dan rather sadly.

"Have you seen all the fabulous quilts that the Village Quilters have on display?" demanded Meadow.

He shook his head slowly, quilt-viewing apparently not on his list of things to do at the fair.

"Then let's head over there," said Meadow in a peremptory tone. "You'll naturally want to see them since you've been spending so much time at the Patchwork Cottage. That way you can see the finished product of what we've all been working on."

So Dan, something of a hostage, was propelled to the quilting booth. On the way, Meadow chatted nonstop with him as Beatrice trailed along, also somewhat of a hostage to Meadow's matchmaking efforts. She felt a bit sorry for Dan as Meadow pulled out her phone to show him the dozens of pictures she had taken of Will on the rides, many of them quite blurry or prominently featuring Meadow's thumb.

When they drew closer to the displays, Beatrice saw Tiggy standing there. Tiggy's eyes widened as she spotted Dan and her hand quickly went to her hair to tidy it.

Meadow said, "Ah, there's Tiggy. Have you met Tiggy, Dan?"

Dan flushed a little. "I believe we spoke briefly when I was working at the shop." He cleared his throat and hesitated. "You were new in town, I believe?"

Tiggy beamed at him. "I'm visiting for now, but am thinking about moving to Dappled Hills. I have family here and I've sort of fallen in love with the town. I love the mountains and the little shops and the people I've met here. I even spoke with a realtor yesterday." She stopped talking abruptly and blushed as if aware she'd been about to launch into a soliloquy.

Dan said slowly, "So this is the first Dappled Hills fair you've attended, then?"

"It is. Although I've been pretty much sticking around the quilt section since I know some of these ladies." Tiggy gave a longing glance toward the lights of the rides and the food trucks.

Dan said with a formal little bow, "Well, it would be my pleasure to escort you around and introduce you to some of my fair favorites. I know all the best food and the rides that are the most fun. That is, if you like rides."

Tiggy gave a gasping laugh. "I don't even know if I like rides or not. We didn't have a fair where I grew up, or my parents didn't take me, either way. So I've never tried them."

Dan's eyes grew big. "Oh, that's a shame. We'll need to have you ride some rides."

Beatrice said, "You might want to start her out on some of the gentler rides." She could just imagine Tiggy on one of those awful spinning rides.

Meadow grinned. "We can highly recommend the carousel. We just saw our grandson become completely obsessed with it and not want to stop riding."

Dan chuckled. "That might be a good idea." He led Tiggy away, pointing to various food trucks and rides and narrating what they were seeing.

Meadow said, "Well, that was my good deed for the day. I don't think I've ever had a more successful attempt at match-making, *ever*."

Chapter Seventeen

"It's early days yet, Meadow. We don't really know if they'll ultimately be suited to each other," cautioned Beatrice.

"Oh, I could tell. There was a spark between them—couldn't you feel it? Anyway, I'm just happy they're starting off on the right foot. Now we can only hope that Dan likes healthy food and doesn't mind wearing homemade clothing. And Savannah and Georgia will be absolutely *delighted*."

Beatrice nodded. "They both do really need some breathing room." She glanced over at the next booth and said, "Let's check in with Posy. Are you still doing all right with your standing?"

"I'm right as rain," said Meadow in a convincing voice.

Posy had her own booth at the fair—a vendor booth for the Patchwork Cottage that had a sample of her fabrics, notions, and patterns. She was apparently getting some good business because she was helping a couple of ladies who'd come over from a neighboring town. Once they had their purchases checked out, she walked over and smiled at Meadow and Beatrice. "How are you enjoying the fair?"

They chatted a few minutes about Will's experience there, Ramsay's award, and Meadows's successful matchmaking.

Posy said, "That all sounds marvelous! A perfect evening."

Beatrice said, "It looks as if things are going well at the Patchwork Cottage booth, too. Have you been getting customers?"

Posy nodded happily. "It's been steady all night. And I've gotten some big orders, too. People from other towns will place orders with me here because they're coming to the fair anyway and don't have a quilt shop where they live. It saves them a trip and gives me sales."

"Wonderful!" said Meadow.

Posy said, "I'm actually thinking about going ahead and starting to pack things up. I'm sure most of my customers have probably already stopped by, especially if they've got a drive ahead of them."

"Where's Cork?" asked Beatrice. Posy's husband ran the local wine shop and was usually the one who helped her with any lugging around she needed to do.

"He's out of town—helping his older brother move into a retirement community. The timing wasn't great, but he really needed to help his brother since he's on his own. It's not a big deal—I'll just take it all down, throw it in the car, and put it in the store."

Someone cleared their throat behind Beatrice and she turned around. Bertha was there. Meadow stared at her with wide eyes as if she were somehow privy to her matchmaking activities and was there to confront her.

Instead, Bertha smiled politely at Beatrice. "Sorry to interrupt. I wanted to ask you if I could maybe skip a cleaning shift at the church that I'd told Edgenora I'd do. Have you seen her here?"

Beatrice shook her head.

Posy said, "I've seen her, but I think she's left for the evening."

Bertha said, "It's just that I have a conflict. I'm real sorry."

Beatrice wondered if the conflict had anything to do with the man Bertha was with at the fair. "I'll mention it to Edgenora. I'm sure we can call in someone else."

"Okay, good. Anyway, I should be meeting up with somebody. Thanks for giving Edgenora the message, Beatrice." She headed off to join her date again, who was standing some yards away.

Posy watched as she walked farther away. "Bertha was acting a little odd earlier. Sort of standoffish. I wondered if she thought I held it against her that she'd broken up with Dan. That I was on Dan's side or something."

Meadow said, "Well, too bad about that! She should have thought of the ramifications if she was going to break up with someone. And Dan's a nice guy."

Posy added slowly, "There was something else, too. While she and I were talking, Miss Sissy came up. She sort of growled at Bertha and stomped away."

"That sounds like usual Miss Sissy behavior," said Beatrice with a laugh.

"Yes. But then Bertha said something like: 'You'd think she'd be in a better mood now that she's getting her quilt back.' I was just surprised that she knew anything about it."

"Do you think Dan might have mentioned the quilt to her? I suppose Dan was around when Miss Sissy was raging about the quilt being stolen," said Meadow.

Beatrice said, "I don't get the impression that Dan was at all interested in any conversations about quilts. Plus, he seems a little deaf. I'm not sure he would have been able to hear Miss Sissy talking about the quilt."

Posy nodded. "I'd agree with you there. I had to use a much-louder voice than usual when I was speaking with him. I did ask Bertha, actually, how she'd heard about the quilt. She probably thought I was being nosy."

"What did she say?" asked Beatrice.

"She said she was cleaning that Sunday Miss Sissy attacked Linton and the windows were open because she was using bleach. Plus, that Miss Sissy was not exactly quiet."

"No, she was yelling at the top of her lungs," said Beatrice ruefully. "Well, that explains it. Although Sunday seems like an odd time to be cleaning."

Posy said, "She said she'd been so busy and in such demand that it was the only time she could make it over to Linton's. Anyway, it's nothing. I just thought Bertha was acting a little off, that's all."

Meadow said, "Going back to you packing up your booth. We can help give you a hand, Posy. You don't need to take this down all by yourself."

Beatrice said, "Meadow, the last thing you need to do is help Posy move. You need to find that bench you were talking about and sit down for a while until Ramsay can leave. I'll help Posy out. And I can volunteer Wyatt, too."

Posy smiled at her. "That's really kind of you. Let's not recruit poor Wyatt, though—you and I should be able to handle it. Because of the sales I've had, there really isn't too much inventory left here."

Meadow chatted for a few more minutes and then headed off to her bench to wait for Ramsay. Posy and Beatrice started taking down Posy's displays and putting them into boxes and tote bags to take to her car.

Beatrice said thoughtfully, "You know, that's very interesting what you said about Bertha."

"Is it?" Posy's face creased with concern. "Oh, dear. I don't mean to say anything bad about Bertha. I just have the feeling she might be very sensitive about Dan and her breakup and perhaps thought I was siding with Dan because he's been at the shop so much."

"No, I mean about the quilt. The fact she knew about it."

"Oh, that. Well, she cleared it up, didn't she? The fact that she was working the Sunday before Linton died and heard his squabble with Miss Sissy," said Posy.

"Yes, but if she was at Linton's house cleaning on Sunday, why was she there the next day?"

"*Was* she there the next day?" asked Posy, confused.

"She says she was. At least, Bertha said she showed up to clean and the police had to wave her away." Beatrice frowned.

Posy said, "Maybe she wasn't finished yet. Or maybe Linton wasn't pleased with the job she'd done and asked her to come back and get the spots she missed."

"That could be the case. But from all accounts and from what I've heard from Edgenora at the church, Bertha is supposed to be a fantastic cleaner. She's in great demand, which is apparently the reason she was working on Sunday." Beatrice carefully lay some of the notions from the shop into a box and taped it up.

Posy said, "That does seem sort of odd, doesn't it? The whole thing seems strange to me, including Bertha's behavior when she and I were speaking. But I don't want to make it look like Bertha had something to hide. Like I said, she might just have been thinking about Dan and wondering if I were blaming her for their breakup."

Beatrice said, "Just the same, I'm going to make a quick call to Ramsay, just to give him a heads-up. It probably doesn't mean anything, like you said, but I'd rather keep him in the loop."

She rang Ramsay's phone, but it went to voicemail, so she left a message. "Hi, it's Beatrice. This is probably nothing, but Posy said Bertha was acting odd tonight. We also heard that she was at Linton's house, cleaning, the Sunday when Miss Sissy and Linton had their argument . . . so why was she back at his house the next day? Anyway, call me when you can, there's no hurry. If I don't pick up, it's because I'm helping Posy take down the booth and take everything back to her store."

Beatrice hung up and then started helping Posy more in earnest. Wyatt came by the booth and offered to help but Posy wouldn't hear of it, saying that he had a busy day the next day since it would be Sunday and it would be best for him to go home and rest—that she would drive Beatrice home after they put everything in the shop. Wyatt said he'd drive Miss Sissy back home since she'd told him she had a bit of a tummy-ache from eating too much fair food.

After Wyatt left with Miss Sissy, Posy and Beatrice loaded Posy's minivan and headed off to the shop. Posy was happily talking about the fair and her sales and looking forward to seeing Cork the next day when he came back from helping his brother.

Posy unlocked the door to the Patchwork Cottage and turned on the lights. Then she and Beatrice unloaded the minivan and brought everything inside.

Posy said, "Well, I think this is enough for one day. I'll sort this out later."

Beatrice looked around at all the boxes and said, "It's going to take you forever, which means you'll have to come in early before the shop opens tomorrow afternoon. Here, I'll help you and it'll cut the time in half."

Posy protested, but Beatrice wouldn't hear of it. Besides, despite feeling tired on one level, Beatrice had the feeling she was too keyed up from the fair to be able to fall asleep if she went back home. She was glad when Posy finally acquiesced and then started opening boxes and totes and finding a home for each item in the shop.

About fifteen minutes later, the bell on the door rang. Posy and Beatrice looked at each other. They were in the middle of the store and concealed by the racks of fabric. "Sorry, we're closed," called out Posy. "Please come back tomorrow afternoon."

The blood drained from Posy's face as they heard Bertha say, "No, I think I'll stay here for now."

Chapter Eighteen

Posy gave Beatrice a wide-eyed look as she stood and then motioned Beatrice to stay down and hidden. Beatrice immediately silenced her phone and then texted Ramsay an SOS, saying where they were and who was there and what was happening. She knew Ramsay was probably still directing exiting traffic at the fair but she hoped he would check his messages. Then she looked through her apps until she found the voice recording one and, with a trembling finger, turned it on.

Posy was saying, "Bertha? What are you doing here? I'm afraid the shop's closed and I'm in the middle of putting everything back."

Bertha said in a saucy voice, "You should learn to lock doors behind you. I know we live in a small town, but bad things can happen in small towns." Her voice held a warning tone that made a shiver go up Beatrice's spine. "Come on over here, Posy. I don't like you standing where I can't see you."

Beatrice glanced around her at the boxes and bags they'd been in the process of unloading. There was a pair of shears but they were still bound up in their packaging and it would be too noisy to unwrap them. Then she spotted the wooden quilt stand that Posy had used to display a quilt outside her booth. She slowly moved nearer to it.

Posy had given a tremulous sigh and walked toward Bertha.

"That's better," said Bertha. Then she added sternly, "It really wasn't like you to be nosy, you know. I don't think of you that way. Being nosy isn't really safe."

Posy acted as if she was confused by what Bertha was saying, trying to draw her out and buy them some time. "Do you mean about your relationship with Dan? I'm sorry if I was nosy. I did feel badly for Dan, though. I couldn't really help it, since he was here working nearly every day. He seemed so deflated when you ended things."

Bertha's voice was frigid and Beatrice grabbed the quilt stand. "Don't be stupid. I'm not talking about Dan. I don't care a thing about him, which is why I dumped him. And I don't care if you're worried about him or not. I'm talking about your nosy questions about Miss Sissy's quilt."

Beatrice stayed hunched over and crept closer to Bertha and Posy, being careful to stay concealed by the fabric displays.

"Nosy questions?" asked Posy faintly. "I'm not sure what you're talking about."

"About Miss Sissy's missing quilt! I could tell by your face that it was obvious you knew something."

Posy asked timidly, "Did *you* take her quilt, Bertha?"

"Of course not! Why would I go lurking in that crazy woman's house? No, I just happened to see that Miss Sissy's quilt was in Linton Hoover's house, that's all."

Posy didn't say anything in return, clearly not wanting to aggravate Bertha more than she already was. Beatrice peered around a display of notions and saw that Bertha's back was facing her. Posy barely glanced her way, not wanting Bertha to know Beatrice was there.

"Well? What have you to say for yourself?" Bertha's hands were on her hips.

Posy said, "That I'm sorry? I'm sorry that you think I've been nosy. I didn't know anything about Miss Sissy's quilt, except that she was upset that it was missing. And I don't understand what it has to do with you."

Beatrice took a couple of quiet steps forward, no longer concealed by the merchandise. In the distance, she could hear the faint sound of a siren.

"That's the whole point! You realized it had something to do with me as soon as *I* mentioned Miss Sissy's quilt. And that's on me—it was just a slip of my tongue after I had those beers with my friend. But you realized I shouldn't know anything about the old woman's missing quilt and now I'm going to have to take care of you like I took care of the others. I could see it all over your face. You're an open book, Posy, you know that? You can't keep your feelings to yourself. I can read your mind by looking at you."

But apparently, Bertha couldn't because Posy's face carefully didn't register a thing when Beatrice brought the wooden quilt stand crashing down on her.

Posy and Beatrice stared at each other and then down at Bertha, who appeared to be out like a light.

"Is she . . . she's not dead, is she?" asked Posy.

Beatrice shook her head. "No, look, she's still breathing. But she's unconscious. I'll check her for a weapon and you find something we can *use* for a weapon in case I can't find something on Bertha. I think that siren is Ramsay—I texted him."

Posy hurried off, returning with some of Dan's painting supplies, including a partially-full can of paint. "Maybe I could swing this at her," said Posy. "It's not too heavy, but heavy enough."

"And I'll hang onto this," said Beatrice, taking a tissue and pulling a gun out of Bertha's pocket. She backed away from her.

The siren was indeed Ramsay and he came barreling into the shop, his own weapon pulled. He called an ambulance when he saw Bertha lying on the floor, the quilt stand broken beside her.

"Here, you take this," said Beatrice, proffering the gun to Ramsay.

Looking grim, he took it in the tissue, flipped the safety on it, and put it on his belt. "Now, could both of you tell me what happened here?"

Beatrice played him the recording as Ramsay handcuffed Bertha, who was now wide awake. She grunted when she saw him, an angry flush crossing her features when she heard her own voice coming from Beatrice's phone. "You tricked me!" she hissed at Posy.

Posy straightened up. "*You* tricked *me*. I was here with Beatrice, who was trying to help me put the merchandise back where it belonged. You pushed your way in here and started all this."

Ramsay frowned. "Let's hear it Bertha. It's only a matter of time, anyway. There's some foreign DNA found on Sandra Hughes. I have the feeling it's going to end up matching yours." He quickly read Bertha her rights.

Bertha set her lips in a furious line. Then she slumped a little. "Why don't you tell me, since you're all so smart. Go ahead, Beatrice, tell me. You couldn't have figured it out too much or Ramsay would have been paying a visit with me before I even came to see Posy."

Ramsay said, "Beatrice did tell me. But I was working the fair and didn't have a chance to check my messages until later. Beatrice said you'd mentioned to Posy that you'd heard Miss Sissy yelling about her missing quilt the Sunday afternoon before Linton died."

"Yeah?" said Bertha.

"Beatrice pointed out that it was weird for you to have returned to Linton's house the following day."

Bertha glared at Beatrice through narrowed eyes. "Weird? I work for the guy."

"You clean weekly for him, though, not daily," said Beatrice. "You realized from Miss Sissy that Linton had stolen her quilt because you saw it in his house while you were cleaning. You went home, thought about it, then decided you'd ask him for money to keep quiet about the quilt."

A look of surprise flashed in Bertha's eyes. She tried to recover by making a scoffing noise. "Me? Try to get money from Linton Hoover? I couldn't even get the guy to pay me on time."

Beatrice looked at Ramsay and he gestured for her to keep going. Beatrice took a deep breath. "Still, you thought it was a money-making opportunity, didn't you? Maybe having something you could hold over him was also a way to make sure he *did* pay you on time in the future. You went to Linton's house early the next morning to tell him he needed to pay you."

Bertha stayed silent, but her eyes were watchful.

"Linton refused to pay you. Maybe he didn't really even have the money you were asking for. He walked away from you and you followed him, still asking for the money. He ended up in his game room and something he said or did made you lose your temper," said Beatrice.

A furrow appeared between Bertha's brows.

"You hit him over the head." Beatrice held out her hands. "Maybe you didn't mean to kill him. Maybe you were just frustrated with him. Regardless, he was dead and you needed to get out of there."

"Listen, plenty of people were mad at Linton Hoover. I've been telling you about them! Anybody could have hit him over the head with a pool cue."

Ramsay said slowly, "I don't believe any of us mentioned that it was a pool cue. It sure is interesting that you know that, though."

A red flush crept up Bertha's neck at her mistake.

Posy gasped. "And Sandra was just going in, right? Sandra was the one who found Linton."

Ramsay took over. "You heard the front door open and Sandra calling out for Linton, right? You didn't want to be found with Linton's dead body, so you left out the back. Your fingerprints were everywhere, but it didn't really matter because we knew you cleaned regularly for him. You thought you'd gotten away with it, didn't you? You were curious about it, though, or worried, so you stopped by a little later acting like you were there to clean and to try to find out what the police knew. But

Sandra had realized you'd been there. Maybe she spotted your car or maybe she saw you out a window as you left."

Bertha said in a vicious voice, "She should never have been there to begin with. She was pushing him into a relationship he didn't want anymore."

"So she saw you. When did she let you know that she'd seen you?" asked Ramsay.

Bertha muttered under her breath and then said, "Just right before she died. Said she was trying to give me a chance to do the right thing and tell the cops what I'd done or seen."

"What you'd seen?" asked Posy with a frown.

Bertha gave her a condescending look. "Sandra wasn't sure if I'd actually killed him. She thought maybe I'd just gone over to clean, saw his body, freaked out, and left and just didn't want to tell the cops I was at the scene."

"But you didn't go to the police," said Ramsay somberly. "So Sandra paid you a visit. Did she come over to your house, then? Is that where she told you that if you didn't go to the cops that she would?"

Bertha gave him a sullen look and Ramsay added, "Remember, there will be DNA evidence."

Bertha shrugged a shoulder and spat out, "That's right. She came over to my house. I wouldn't have even let her in if I'd known what she was there for. She sort of shoved her way in like the pushy person she was. Then she said, all prim and proper, that if I weren't going to 'inform law enforcement of my proximity to Linton' when he died, that she was going to."

Ramsay was still for a moment and then said, "So you killed her. Hit her on the back of the head with a hard object. What was the object?"

Posy, always a sensitive soul, gave a soft, sad sigh.

"A paperweight," said Bertha between gritted teeth.

Beatrice shook her head. "And you dragged her out of there all by yourself? The dead body of a grown woman?"

Bertha shot her a look. "Are you kidding me? I'm no weakling. In this job, you've got to be strong and have endurance. I just parked my car close to the house, opened the trunk, then picked her up and tossed her in."

"Which is obviously what you did at the lake," said Ramsay.

Bertha made a face. "Well, I should have weighed her down. My mistake. But she was heavy enough as it was, even with me being used to hauling things around."

"Then tonight," said Ramsay. "You trying to get rid of Posy was pretty well explained on the recording Beatrice made. You saw her at the fair, thought she knew something because of the quilt, and then decided to follow her to the shop to get rid of her."

Bertha countered, "I didn't *follow* her. I heard her say that Cork wasn't in town and she'd be taking the stuff back to her shop, herself. If I'd *followed* her, I'd have realized she had Beatrice there with her and I wouldn't have gone in." She gave Posy a sour look. "If you'd just locked the door, this wouldn't have happened at all."

Ramsay sighed. "Yes, I think we all need to remember to do a better job locking our doors. If Miss Sissy had locked hers, the quilt never would have ended up in Linton's house to begin with." He said, "Okay, Bertha, it's time for us to head to the station and for me to get the state police caught up. Let's head out."

They started out and then Ramsay's eyes grew big. "Oh, no. Meadow! I was supposed to take her home."

"We'll pick her up and take her home," said Posy quickly.

After Ramsay and Bertha left, Beatrice and Posy stared at each other for a moment before Posy gave Beatrice a fierce hug. "Beatrice, if you hadn't offered to help me out, I'd have been another victim."

"I'm just glad you mentioned that Cork was out of town or I wouldn't have been here." A shiver rose up Beatrice's spine at the thought.

"I called him to fill him in a few minutes ago. He said he'd be coming home as soon as possible. Now, let's go home," said Posy suddenly. "We've done a lot of the unpacking and I'll tackle the rest tomorrow. I don't think I have the energy to do any more tonight."

"I think you should call Minerva and have her open the store tomorrow. Give yourself the chance to sleep in."

Posy gave a rueful laugh. "If I can even get to sleep after this."

"I'm still keyed up, myself. How about if you join Wyatt and me for a glass of wine, some time with Noo-noo, and a short visit first?"

So Posy did, right after they dropped off an excited and indignant Meadow by her house. Beatrice invited Meadow to come in, but was rather relieved to hear that Meadow did want to rest her foot. Posy and Beatrice caught Wyatt up on what happened and then carefully changed the subject to pets, quilting, and music and the stress of the evening and being with friends started falling away. When Posy left a while later, she had a smile on her face again.

The next afternoon, after church, Beatrice was again taking a little nap. Wyatt was working assiduously on his crossword and doing a lot of erasing and rewriting. They both started as they heard a shriek, reminding them of Miss Sissy's the last time they'd been relaxing like that. But then Beatrice smiled because it was a happy shriek this time. She headed back to the bedroom to get Will, who grinned at her as he was waking up from his own nap.

About the Author:

Elizabeth writes the Southern Quilting mysteries and Memphis Barbeque mysteries for Penguin Random House and the Myrtle Clover series for Midnight Ink and independently. She blogs at ElizabethSpannCraig.com/blog, named by Writer's Digest as one of the 101 Best Websites for Writers. Elizabeth makes her home in Matthews, North Carolina, with her husband. She's the mother of two.

Sign up for Elizabeth's free newsletter to stay updated on releases:

https://bit.ly/2xZUXqO

This and That

I love hearing from my readers. You can find me on Facebook as Elizabeth Spann Craig Author, on Twitter as elizabethscraig, on my website at elizabethspanncraig.com, and by email at elizabethspanncraig@gmail.com.

A special thanks to John DeMeo and Karen Young for their support!

Thanks so much for reading my book...I appreciate it. If you enjoyed the story, would you please leave a short review on the site where you purchased it? Just a few words would be great. Not only do I feel encouraged reading them, but they also help other readers discover my books. Thank you!

Did you know my books are available in print and ebook formats? Most of the Myrtle Clover series is available in audio and some of the Southern Quilting mysteries are. Find the audiobooks here.

Please follow me on BookBub for my reading recommendations and release notifications.

I'd also like to thank some folks who helped me put this book together. Thanks to my cover designer, Karri Klawiter, for her awesome covers. Thanks to my editor, Judy Beatty for her help. Thanks to beta readers Amanda Arrieta, Rebecca Wahr, and Dan Harris for all of their helpful suggestions and careful reading. Thanks to my ARC readers for helping to spread the word. Thanks, as always, to my family and readers.

Other Works by Elizabeth:

Myrtle Clover Series in Order (be sure to look for the Myrtle series in audio, ebook, and print):

Pretty is as Pretty Dies

Progressive Dinner Deadly

A Dyeing Shame

A Body in the Backyard

Death at a Drop-In

A Body at Book Club

Death Pays a Visit

A Body at Bunco

Murder on Opening Night

Cruising for Murder

Cooking is Murder

A Body in the Trunk

Cleaning is Murder

Edit to Death

Hushed Up

A Body in the Attic

Murder on the Ballot

Death of a Suitor (2021)

Southern Quilting Mysteries in Order:
Quilt or Innocence
Knot What it Seams
Quilt Trip
Shear Trouble
Tying the Knot
Patch of Trouble
Fall to Pieces
Rest in Pieces
On Pins and Needles
Fit to be Tied
Embroidering the Truth
Knot a Clue
Quilt-Ridden
The Village Library Mysteries in Order (Debuting 2019):
Checked Out
Overdue
Borrowed Time
Hush-Hush
Where There's a Will (2021)
Memphis Barbeque Mysteries in Order (Written as Riley Adams):
Delicious and Suspicious
Finger Lickin' Dead
Hickory Smoked Homicide
Rubbed Out
And a standalone "cozy zombie" novel: Race to Refuge, written as Liz Craig

Printed in the USA
CPSIA information can be obtained
at www.ICGtesting.com
LVHW010924210724
786093LV00030B/790

9 781946 227959